*"I knew you'd be a hot little thing,
all that simmering heat just barely glossed over
with a façade of coolness."*

Fallon flushed deeply. How could he know the fantasies that invaded her dreams, as well as her waking hours? The images of unclothed limbs entwined. Sex-sweat damp bodies. Moans and cries, and carnal delights she would never know. How, in mere minutes, had he discovered her secret?

She attempted to pull away, but succeeded only in inflaming things further. Squirming in his lap, she felt him harden. "Please," she said on a breathy sigh. "It's not right."

"Give me a second," Bridge said throatily. "I promise you I'll make it right."

Taboo

Kathleen Lawless

POCKET BOOKS

New York London Toronto Sydney Singapore

POCKET BOOKS, a division of Simon & Schuster, Inc.
1230 Avenue of the Americas, New York, NY 10020

ISBN: 0-7434-7671-9

First Pocket Books trade paperback edition October 2003

10 9 8 7 6 5 4 3 2 1

Manufactured in the United States of America

For information regarding special discounts for bulk purchases,
please contact Simon & Schuster Special Sales
at 1-800-456-6798 or business@simonandschuster.com

Dedicated to my three wonderful, talented,
and amazing children

Acknowledgment

Special thanks to brainstorming mavin Jennifer T.
for her generosity with her time and creativity

ta•boo: *adj* (1777) proscribed by society as improper and unacceptable

Chapter One

Fallon Gilchrist reread the hastily scrawled note that had been delivered that morning, smiling at her best friend's childishly rounded handwriting.

Darling, Anna wrote, *you've been cooped up alone in the middle of nowhere for far too long. I'm arriving to relieve your tedium. And bringing along a very big surprise. Love and kisses.*

Fallon felt her smile fade to pensiveness as she refolded the note. Anna's sense of excitement and daring seemed to leap right off the page and into her lonely drawing room. Perhaps her best friend was right. Perhaps she had been sequestered in the country for too long.

After leaving orders with her housekeeper that Anna's favorite room be made ready, Fallon headed outside to her studio. Perhaps, while the light was good, she'd find the inspiration she sought. The inspiration that had so eluded her of late.

She paused halfway between manor house and studio and studied the converted gatehouse, her favorite haven on the estate. It had been her late husband's surprise to her, fashioning the estate's gatehouse into a place where she might give free rein to her artistic passions.

Powell had never guessed at the sexual passions Fallon took pains to keep hidden. Surely it wasn't normal to have one's thoughts consumed by the sex act between man and woman. She'd married Powell convinced that his maturing years would afford her a lifetime partner who knew how to satisfy her womanly needs. Instead, he had seemed quite taken aback by her initial enthusiasm, so she had learned to please him, to act demure. In need of coaxing. Apparently, proper ladies did not crave their husband's touch, but suffered through it. At any rate, her disappointment when his efforts failed to inflame her or provide release only mounted, and she'd taken up painting, a poor but acceptable outlet for some of her pent-up sexual frustration.

Except, lately, her work felt flat. She no longer derived satisfaction from her painting. The play of light and shadow on canvas no longer stirred her senses. How well she recalled the time when the scent of turpentine and linseed oil, the array of half-squeezed paint tubes, the texture of the paints themselves left her positively light-headed. In those days she fairly chafed to get to her work. To feel that heightened sensation stream through her veins in a rush like no other, until the climax was achieved, as all those feelings churning inside her spilled forth onto the canvas.

Nowadays she ventured to her studio more from habit than from desire. She spent an inordinate amount of time cleaning and organizing her sable-hair paintbrushes, lining up her tubes of color perfectly, trying to decide if they should be grouped into color families or be alphabetized. On days when she felt energetic, she would even stretch and prime a new canvas in preparation.

She unlocked the door and let out a sigh as she stepped inside. The canvas might be ready, but was she? The vase of fresh peonies she had arranged yesterday was even more perfect today. Heavy heads nodded and drooped as if half asleep. She leaned close and inhaled their delicate yet distinctive fragrance. June in Boston. More than a dozen shades of pink all vied for attention, yet ultimately failed to inspire her. How sad that she couldn't muster the energy even to open her paints, let alone create the perfect shades.

Had she always been this melancholy? Powell used to remark how she could bring a smile to his face, no matter what. Surely she hadn't always felt so weighted down, so heavy in her heart.

Powell and his architect had removed the entire south-facing wall of the former gatehouse and replaced it with panes of glass. Fallon watched the leaden-gray sky darken, then turned and made her way to an elaborate wrought-iron candelabra. Powell had been astute enough to understand the importance of light to an artist, thus the studio had been fitted with an excess of sconces, gaslights, lanterns, and candles. Even now, a year after his death, she missed her husband's thoughtful kindness.

She'd always felt faintly guilty that she didn't love him as deeply as he loved her. Oh, she'd cared for him. He'd been a kind and thoughtful husband, aware that she'd married him for the security he could provide her in her orphaned state. And she'd refrained from taking a lover the way so many of her Boston friends had. Even when Powell was away at sea for months on end, and numbing sleep eluded her. How many nights had she lain awake, restless, unfulfilled longings burning deep inside her? Longings that she suspected a lover, the right lover, would be able to satisfy.

She struck a match and lit a candle. It sputtered and caught the wick. Fallon stared, mesmerized. She reached out and felt its faint heat, both feeble and hot enough to burn, then snatched back her hand. What on earth was coming over her? Thank goodness for Anna's note, giving her something to look forward to.

She heard a faint commotion outside. Could her friend have arrived already?

Across the room, the studio door burst open. "Darling!" Anna never simply entered a room, she took over the room, and this visit proved no exception. Fallon found herself enveloped in her friend's embrace and soundly hugged before Anna pulled back and eyed her critically. "You're too thin," she announced. "Hasn't Mrs. Buttle been feeding you?"

Fallon shrugged and shifted the attention from herself. "Now that you're here, cook will prepare anything you fancy. I've had your room made ready."

"Sweetheart." Anna made a moue of regret. "Sorry, but I'm unable to stay. I'm only here to deliver your surprise."

"What have you been up to now?" Fallon asked fondly.

"Wait till you see." Anna giggled girlishly, her excitement contagious. She clapped her hands loudly and her manservant appeared in the doorway with a second young man in tow.

Fallon's breath caught in her throat. Despite the silk scarf secured blindfold-style across the stranger's eyes, she could tell he was a creature of inordinate beauty. At a gesture from Anna, the manservant withdrew. Anna winked at the speechless Fallon and unwound the scarf.

"Montague Bridgeman, meet your new mistress, Fallon Gilchrist."

"Anna." Fallon frowned, conveying her dismay and disapproval.

"It's all right, darling. He's bought and paid for. Yours for half a fortnight. Isn't that so, Montague?"

The young man stepped forward and bowed. A thick lock of dark hair fell rakishly across his forehead with the movement. "Your servant, madam. As your friend rightly proclaimed, I am yours to command as you wish for seven days and seven nights."

The man before Fallon was truly a most exquisite creature. Beneath his finely cut jacket, she could discern the way his broad shoulders tapered to a narrow waist and hips. His strong legs were encased in well-cut fitted trousers. But as Fallon gazed up at him, his eyes were her undoing. Brooding. Haunted. Jaded. Worldly-wise and tired. The wrong eyes for so young a face, yet perfect nonetheless. Those eyes held volumes. Sound and silence. Life and death. And Fallon knew she had to paint them, to capture their story. To reveal their owner's soul. Her fingers fairly itched to pick up a brush and begin.

It felt as if a lifetime sped past while their gazes locked, yet she knew it could have been no longer than seconds.

"I'm afraid I don't understand."

"It's simple, my dear. The Boston Women's Auxiliary is raising funds to buy more books for the library. One of our members decided we should have an auction. One with a truly exceptional prize."

"Madam, you flatter me overmuch."

"The second I laid eyes on Montague, I knew I must secure him for you. All the ladies wanted him, of course, but I knew I had to get him for you—no matter what the price. Happy birthday!"

"Anna," Fallon said, "you should know me well enough to know I shan't be party to this."

Anna pulled Fallon aside. Very gently she laid one gloved hand against Fallon's cheek. "I miss the old Fallon. My friend. I want her back."

Fallon was humbled by the sincerity in her friend's gaze, her touch. "I miss her, too."

"I know you do. Which is why I've gone to such extreme lengths to awaken you from this stupor you seem to have fallen victim to. Montague has no clue who you are or where he is. I shall return in seven days' time to take him back to the city."

"It's outrageous."

Anna's gaze left Fallon to fasten upon her young companion. "Tell me you don't long to paint him. That face. Those eyes. That hair."

"Of course I long to paint him. . . ."

"Then do it," Anna said briskly. "Wake up and rejoin the world." She turned abruptly. "One week. I expect you to get my money's worth for me."

Anna's departure left Fallon alone in the studio with her "surprise."

"So that's it, then? It's down to you and me?" He didn't sound overly pleased by the prospect. For that matter, neither was she.

"So it would seem." Fallon circled him slowly, assessingly, as one might a prize stallion offered for sale. Yet in this case the sale had been completed. He stood before her, primed to do her bidding. Or was he?

"How well do you take orders?"

"As well as any former soldier."

Fallon was unsure if his words meant he was adept at following orders or if he had long ago had his fill of it.

"You look too young to have been to war."

"Every man, no matter his age, is too young to go to war."

That one terse comment helped explain those fascinating eyes. And made her long all the more to paint him.

His very stance indicated excellent lineage, hands clasped loosely behind his back, his pose straight yet seeming coiled with energy. How could he appear to lounge, yet stand ready to spring at the same time? She sensed a slight indolence, as if he were bored already, despite the obvious habit of good posture, squared shoulders, and a cocky tilt to his splendidly shaped head.

One unruly lock of hair insisted on falling across his forehead and into his eyes, and Fallon resisted the urge to smooth it aside. She suspected it was as much a part of him as the square jaw, chiseled cheekbones, and magnificent, nearly black, storm-filled eyes.

"Does the lady find me to her liking?" His voice seemed to resonate from someplace deep inside, rich and provocatively masculine. Fallon felt the hair on the back of her neck prickle in awareness.

"Too soon to know," she said crisply as she continued her perusal. She would start by sketching him. Broad charcoal strokes to capture his bold stance and stare. She moved closer. Excellent. He had a faint cleft in his chin. Full, sensual lips that on a less masculine man would be in danger of appearing effeminate, yet on him, saved him from appearing too predatory.

Fallon paused directly in front of him. "May I please see your hands?"

"My hands, my lady?" Faint amusement at her request was indicated by the slight lifting of one brow. "Surely there are other parts of my anatomy you'd find of infinitely more interest than my hands?"

"You heard my request." She returned his gaze squarely. Watched him shift his weight.

"The left or the right?"

"Either," Fallon said pleasantly.

"You choose." There was a challenge, both in the way he

said it and in the accompanying movement as he flexed first his left shoulder her way, then his right.

With a start, Fallon realized that she was enjoying meeting his challenge. A kind of nonverbal sparring. "I say . . ." She paused, ran a hand flat-palmed up his left upper arm, then his right. She could feel his body heat through the fine worsted of his jacket. "I say the right. Are you right-handed, Montague?"

"Bridge." As he spoke he extended his right hand and arm, allowing the tips of his fingers to brush, ever so lightly, the fine bones of her wrist.

"Bridge?" She was confused, both by his words and his touch. Was he offering to build a bridge between them?

"I prefer being addressed as Bridge," he said. "I find it more distinctive. And since we shall be together night and day for an entire half a fortnight . . ."

She shivered at his words, at the intent she saw in his eyes. "Night and day?"

"That was the agreed-upon arrangement."

She tore her gaze from his to focus on his hand. Long, strong fingers, large knuckles, a broad, capable palm. Definitely a man's hand. Square-cut nails, clean but not buffed. Faint calluses, from riding, no doubt. Or perhaps fencing. She nodded in approval.

"My turn." He captured her hand in his and turned it over in thoughtful contemplation. She endeavored to see herself through his eyes. How pale and white her skin looked next to his. How small and delicate her fingers. And the way he stroked her palm, eliciting a faint frisson of awareness that seemed to snake up her arm, tingle her breasts, and flutter down low in her feminine recesses.

Fallon attempted to pull free. His grip tightened. Slowly, inexorably, he drew her hand up near his lips. She felt the warmth of his breath, captured his intent seconds before his lips and tongue made contact with her palm.

"Oh, my." Did she say the words aloud or simply think them? It was a snakebite with none of the venom, yet it carried a jolt of shock. Warm and questing, just like her captor, who clearly knew exactly what he was doing. Was he equally aware of her reaction?

How could he not be? How could he fail to recognize the catch in her breath? The increase in her heartbeat? The faint flush marring her skin? She felt her nipples tighten against the front of her gown and prayed that he couldn't see what she felt. Prickles of moisture beaded up and down the length of her legs. The banks of her womanhood softened, damp with anticipation. The feelings, infinitely familiar, were heightened tenfold in her companion's presence.

With a sense of relief, she realized he had ceased tracing circles on her palm with the tip of his tongue. It was a double relief to be able to speak in normal tones as she rescued her hand from his warm, intimate embrace.

"Tell me. What manner of man allows his services to be auctioned to the highest bidder?"

He shrugged. "I had no other pressing commitments for the week. Besides, it struck me as being a worthy cause."

"Why not just make a donation to that worthy cause?"

He smiled, the first genuine smile she'd seen from him. It

deepened the cleft in his chin and lightened the weight in those eyes. "I like not knowing what shall happen next."

Ah, a thrill seeker. A man who thrives on risk. "In that case, I fear you're due to be disappointed. I live very simply and quietly."

His widening grin served only to discomfit her further. "I'm always open to new experiences. Which is precisely why I'm here."

Chapter Two

Where had his impetuousness led him this time? Bridge wondered. For a certainty, the blindfolded carriage ride had served as tantalizing fodder for his vivid imagination and kindled his expectations for the upcoming week. But the lively woman who had secured his services at the auction had now divested herself of him, leaving him in the company of this tall, cool ice princess. Everything about the woman before him appeared tinged with frost, from her silver blue eyes to hair so pale blond as to be nearly silver. She wore it pulled back from her cameo-perfect face, not a single hair out of place. For now. Bridge smiled inwardly. Warming her up could prove to be a good bit of fun. In his considerable experience, those women who appeared outwardly icy tended to have the hottest core.

"Where, exactly, are we?" Was it his imagination or did she pinken slightly at the boldness of his gaze?

"You hardly need concern yourself with such trifling details," she replied haughtily.

"I meant this room, which is most curious in its appointments. I trust it's to be my abode for the next seven days?"

She worried her full lower lip slightly before giving a jerky nod of agreement.

He stretched, arms toward the ceiling. Might as well make himself at home, then. "I shall require a hot bath. It was a devilish long carriage ride to get here." She smiled, and he wondered what he had said to give her amusement.

"I shall see to the bath later," she said. "First, you're to earn your keep. Kindly disrobe, if you please."

Now *that* was more like it. Bridge shrugged out of his jacket and started on the pearl buttons fronting his shirt. He didn't see a bed anyplace. The settee, pushed off to one side, would no doubt serve. Unless perhaps the lady liked it standing up. Or bent over a table. Or . . .

As he unfastened his trousers he licked his lips, envisioning the limitless prospects afforded by the unconventional surroundings. Yes, indeed. This adventure could prove very much to his liking.

She was staring at him, seeming entranced, as he doffed his shirt. No doubt she was saddled with a neglectful husband, off seeing to other pursuits. As well as other women. Bridge sat down to remove his boots and stockings, then paused, leaned back on the settee, and extended one booted foot her way.

"Some women prefer to help."

"You strike me as being eminently capable."

"In many ways, as you shall find out," Bridge replied. "Shall I light the fire?"

"Later, perhaps." She paced before him as she spoke, her eyes glowing and her cheeks flushed with excitement or anticipation, perhaps both, as she observed him from different angles. Animation gave her features an unusual beauty.

"I'm honored that you think me, alone, capable of keeping you warm. However, I do enjoy the experience of fucking before a crackling fire. Don't you?"

She halted in midstride and drew herself erect. "You clearly have the wrong impression of the type of service I require."

Hadn't he heard that one before? Come to think of it, what hadn't he heard?

"I need the settee moved closer to the windows. Facing like so." She indicated her wishes with a graceful wave of her hands.

"Britches on or off for the job?" Bridge inquired.

"Please yourself."

Off, then. Quickly Bridge added his trousers to the tidy pile of his discarded clothing, aware that he cut a dashing figure, with or without the latest style draping his frame. But as he repositioned the settee as ordered, he was chagrined that she hadn't really seemed to notice. Instead, she appeared to be fussing with several lengths of cloth across the room. He settled himself on the settee to wait.

She turned and started toward him, a bundle of claret-colored velvet in her arms, then let out a startled cry at the sight of him draped decorously on the furniture.

His cock responded the way it always did when a beautiful woman was in the room. "There, now. Is this what you had in mind?"

"It's a start, at least," Fallon said, appearing to recover herself. "Kindly rise for a moment. I wish to lay this fabric beneath you."

And I want to lay you beneath me. Bridge rose and watched as she draped the fabric just so, tucking and bunching it in some spots, smoothing it in others. Why did she even bother when they were about to mess it up? Eventually she straightened, seeming satisfied with her efforts.

"I think that will do." Again, a graceful wave of her hand. "As you were."

"I'll need a little help with that," Bridge said as he resumed his pose. For his cock had deflated due to lack of attention. "Why don't you come over here and make me hard?"

"I actually prefer you flaccid for the time being."

"Can't promise to stay that way for long," Bridge said cheerfully. He was as good as his word, his member beginning to stir the second she moved closer. He could smell her heat, her slightly moist skin, her fragrance. Most of all, he could smell her excitement. That universal female smell of a woman aroused by passion.

"One of us is wearing entirely too many articles of clothing," he murmured. As she leaned in he reached toward her, attempting to pull her down upon him.

"Don't move," she snapped, smartly batting his hand away. "Don't you dare move a muscle until I say you can."

"So that's how it is to be played, then?"

She raked her fingers through his hair, and the feel of her nails against his scalp served to excite him further. He'd been tied up and ravaged a time or two, but never forced to hold a pose for an extended period of time. "How long do you expect me to sit like this?"

"As long as it takes," she said. "Now, if you would be so good as to stop talking and allow me to concentrate." To his amazement and disbelief, she reached for a block of white paper and an unwieldy-looking chunk of charcoal and proceeded to sketch him.

He truly *was* a magnificent male animal. A virile combination of outward domestication, yet obviously still half wild inside. Untamed and untamable beneath the thin veneer of civilized behavior. Fallon's hand moved without hesitation as she filled sheet after sheet of paper till the floor around her was littered. She'd never sketched the human form before, having restricted herself to still lifes and landscapes. My word, what she had missed. A living, breathing form with its definition of muscle and sinew, light and shadow, skin and hair.

She recalled the controversy generated by artists William Rimmer and William Morris Hunt, who offered classes for women that included life drawing. She had heard rumors that the female students were criticized and praised as frankly as any man, and wondered how that might feel. She had opted for safety, herself. Still lifes and landscapes and no one to criticize her work, save herself.

Until now. And the pulse of raw, primal power surging through her. As if she had been born for no other purpose than the chance to capture the likeness of the man before her. Her blood sang and danced through her veins. She had never felt so inspired, so tapped in to her passions.

Fallon sketched tirelessly until her hand abruptly spasmed with a cramp. She ignored it and pressed on, frenzied haste in her movements. The light was changing. Her eye saw but her hand refused to do her bidding, and the charcoal tumbled from her fingers to land at her feet. Reluctantly she laid aside her sketching block. She was primed. Tomorrow she would start using color.

"May I move now?"

"Of course. I'm so sorry." Fallon stood, flexing her fingers to restore the blood flow, instantly contrite. If she was experiencing a cramped hand, think how her subject must feel.

"I'm afraid I'm going to need some help." He grimaced as he spoke.

"I do apologize. I'm afraid I haven't been so focused, or so inspired, in a very long time." Several long strides brought her to his side, where she took hold of his arm and began to lightly massage the muscles stretching from forearm to elbow to upper arm to shoulder. She could feel the power beneath her touch.

"Is that better?" she asked anxiously. What if she'd worked him too hard, to the point where he was unable to pose for her tomorrow?

"Somewhat." He struggled from his half recline to a fully seated position. Fallon tugged on his arm, attempting to help, unprepared for his playful tug back, which toppled her into his lap.

"There, now. My turn to pose you." He rearranged a dampened tendril of hair that curled near her brow. "You smell delicious." His words, a slight rumble in her ear, were followed by the wet warmth of his open mouth against the sensitive skin just below her earlobe.

His other arm rested comfortably around her midsection near her breasts, which had begun to tingle in a most distracting way. Even through the modest folds of her brocade gown and layers of underpinnings, she felt a masculine stirring beneath her.

Her nether regions responded in a most unmistakable, shocking way. Waves of heat rippled through her, followed by a trickle of moisture from her heated female core.

He continued to lave her neck, seeking the responsive dip between shoulder and neck, following it to the sensitive nape, one finger burrowing beneath the neckline of her prim gown. At the same time, his hand around her midriff quested upward, strong, capable fingers rubbing the hardened nubs of her nipples. She gasped softly in relief.

Never before had she felt as if her nipples were attached directly to her inner sanctum, but the piercing rush of heat from one to the other was accompanied by a flood of liquid from that wellspring of femininity.

"I knew you'd be a hot little thing—all that simmering heat just barely glossed over with a façade of coolness."

Fallon flushed more deeply. How could he know the fantasies that invaded her dreams, as well as her waking hours?

The images of unclothed limbs entwined. Sex-sweat damp bodies. Moans and cries and . . . Carnal delights she would never know. But imagine them, she did, to the best of her limited knowledge. How, in mere minutes, had Bridge discovered her secret?

As she attempted to pull away, she succeeded only in inflaming things further. Squirming in his lap, she felt his cock harden and lengthen with each slight movement, and her body responded with a melting wetness.

"Don't pretend you're not wet," he said. "I can feel it." He pinched one nipple lightly as he spoke and Fallon heard herself whimper helplessly. Wanting, needing more.

"Open your legs. That's it." Impatiently he pushed her skirt out of the way. She felt the cool air of the room against the overheated skin of her inner thighs. He probed her slit through her damp knickers, knowing fingers teasing her overheated flesh.

"Please," Fallon said, on a breathy sigh. "It's not right."

"Give me a second," Bridge said throatily. "I promise you I'll make it right." As he spoke, he slipped a finger beneath her lace-trimmed knickers. Such a contrast, his callused finger pad on her soft flesh. His cool skin against her heat. His dry finger now moist from her juices. With unerring aim he parted the weeping, pouting lips. Fallon sighed in pleasure. Had anything *ever* felt quite so wonderful as the pressure of his fingers? Now two, now three, teasing, tantalizing, torturing . . .

As the tip of one digit brushed her clitoris, Fallon screamed, and her spine arched as blessed release hit like a wave, swamping her limbs and rendering her limp in Bridge's lap.

"Feel better now, I'll wager," Bridge remarked as her breathing gradually returned to near normal.

She didn't answer as she rearranged her clothing and pushed herself unsteadily to her feet, careful to keep her eyes averted from the swollen redness of his immense erection. Knowing, even as she moved away, how wonderful it would be to feel that fabulous cock embedded deep inside her.

"Where are you going?"

"To order you a bath. Along with some supper."

"Order up a bottle of wine while you're about it, would you?" Bridge rose and stretched, his magnificent cock ramrod straight in front of him.

Never before had Fallon considered the male form to be such an object of beauty. Her own body, sated or not, responded to the sight in a manner so basic that it shocked her. Primal want. Her insides wept just anticipating their joining. His possession of her? Or her possession of him?

Until now, she'd suspected but not fully realized Powell's lack of knowledge about the female anatomy and its workings. Doubtless Bridge had serviced a great many women over the years, to be so proficient and yet so totally controlled.

Even to consider an affair with him was sheer folly. He was years her junior, even if his sexual capabilities were far advanced. And any man who would allow himself to be bought and sold was clearly without scruples. It was up to her to ensure they had no further physical contact. She would keep things between them pleasant, yet distant. She would capture his likeness, that was all.

Yet, as she made her way from the studio to the main house, she was already planning a series of delicacies for the upcoming meal, aware of the contentment rippling through her, her limbs relaxed, her stride easy. A lovely, tingly glow reminded her that Bridge was there for seven full days and seven full nights.

Chapter Three

Fallon deliberately delayed her return to the studio. She didn't want to give her guest the impression that she could scarcely stay away. On the contrary, she was the lady of the manor, with all the responsibilities that accompanied that station. Unlike Bridge, who appeared to have neither responsibilities nor a sense of propriety.

Had he still been bathing he'd be shriveled and frozen to the core. She found him neither. In fact, he'd made himself quite at home, having lit the fire along with several lanterns, which lent the studio a homey glow.

He had also pulled out a good dozen or more of her completed paintings and lined them up side by side along the studio wall. The sight stopped her cold. She'd never looked upon her work all of a piece. Frowning at his forwardness, she advanced to where he lolled against a table, a glass of ruby-colored claret balanced in his hand as if it belonged there.

He'd changed into dove-gray trousers—snugly fastened, she was happy to see—and a crisp white linen shirt that was only partially buttoned, baring more than a tease of his splendidly sculpted chest. Her frown was wasted. He didn't even glance up at her entrance, but continued to study her work.

"You're not half bad," he said, as if his opinion carried weight. "I prefer your earlier works. Less controlled, even if the technique is a little less polished. The more recent ones strike me as somewhat too careful. Artists need to take risks if they're to grow."

When had she last taken a risk? "Are you an art critic, as well as a wastrel?"

Two servants followed her inside, set the trays of food on a low table near the fire, and left. Judging from his cocky grin and the near-empty wine bottle, it was a good thing she'd arrived with food.

"Just what makes you think I'm a wastrel?"

"If you had responsibilities the way the rest of us do, you'd not be available for the type of shenanigans you've embarked upon."

He cocked a brow. "And here I rather thought you enjoyed our earlier shenanigans."

She abruptly changed the subject as she lifted the silver

covers from the serving dishes. "I put my work away for a reason."

He sauntered over to join her. "You're hiding."

She forced back a laugh that sounded hollow, even to her. "I'm hardly hiding."

"You've not been making the social rounds in the city. I'd have remembered you."

"I prefer to devote myself to my work and my responsibilities. Unlike yourself."

He picked up a baked oyster on the half-shell and devoured it in a single bite. "You don't know a single thing about me. Why judge? Or presume?"

"What makes you think I care to know anything about you?"

He laughed and reached for a second oyster, brushing her arm most deliberately, it seemed. "My dear Fallon. May I call you Fallon? It's a name which suits you most splendidly." At her reluctant nod, he continued. "Up until now, you've only painted safe subject matter."

"You're hardly to be considered a safe subject."

"And now, neither are you. For you and I are both aware you need to get to know the 'me,' inside as well as out. Only then will you be able to capture my true essence."

"What makes you think I even want to capture your true essence?"

"Every artist longs to capture his subject's true essence. The ability to do so is what separates the good from the truly great."

"You speak as if you have knowledge on the subject."

"If I'm an artist, then I'm an artist of humanity in general. Flawed. Driven. Bound to disappoint. People are my medium, as paint and canvas is yours. Shall we eat before the food grows cold?"

"Of course." Fallon had been so caught up listening to him that all else had receded from her mind, including social pleasantries and food. He had a very real depth, surprising in one so young. And, much as she hated to admit it, he was right on a number of scores.

"Oysters. Quail. Trout." Bridge lifted covers and inhaled with great gusto. "I applaud your choices. Food to be eaten with the fingers further stir the senses."

Oh, dear. Was that what she'd been thinking when she'd conferred with cook?

"I wasn't sure as to your tastes."

"You chose well. I consider food to be one of life's many delightful sensory experiences. Come, let us eat before the fire."

"I'm not—"

"I'm yours for seven days only. And you know I speak the truth. You do need to know me, from the soul out."

"I'm rather surprised to hear you haven't yet sold your soul to the devil."

He responded with a satanic grin. "Perhaps I have. That, too, is something you must discern." He splashed some wine into a goblet and placed it before her, then refilled his glass, which he raised in a toast. "To the lady Fallon. And the mysteries she is sure to uncover."

She cocked her head, studying him. "You have a rather inflated opinion of yourself."

"Modesty was never one of my flaws. Nor circumspection." Ripping a chunk of meat from the quail, he raised it to her lips. His grease-covered pinkie finger nudged her lips apart, and he slid the morsel into her mouth in a move that seemed even more intimate than the way he had touched her earlier.

Fallon was too shocked to do anything other than chew. She only hoped she'd be able to swallow. The sight of Bridge sucking each finger clean triggered a strange tugging sensation in her womb. She swallowed with difficulty. "You have a napkin, you know."

He glanced down lazily. "So I do. Your turn to feed me."

How had he done that? She could well imagine herself feeding him the way he had fed her. Her fingers tingled, imagining his strong lips sucking the juices from her skin, ravaging her palm the way he had earlier. She pushed her plate aside and clasped her hands tightly together in her lap, safe from temptation.

"I do believe I challenge you," he said.

"Painting you shall be quite enough of a challenge, thank you."

"Painting me is a safe challenge. The other—"

"There is no other," she said.

"That's where you're mistaken. The other challenge is the real one. The unsafe one. And the one with the greater reward." He cocked a look. "You've hardly touched your meal."

"I'm not hungry. The hour grows late and I want to get an early start in the morning."

"Perhaps you're too excited to eat," he suggested. "Anticipating the unfolding of the next seven days?"

She rose. "Don't drink all that wine. I want you clear-headed and well rested in the morning."

He rose as well. "You shall have me any way you want me."

She crossed the room, aware of his eyes following her, riveted on the sway of her hips and the rounded curve of her bottom beneath her skirt. She paused, one hand on the studio door, and turned. "I want honesty between us always. What you said earlier was true. I need to know the man inside, to probe below the surface to do you full justice."

Three long strides brought him to her side. "I am an onion, to be peeled back layer after layer. I only appear transparent. I shan't make it easy. But I never lie."

His closeness should have felt stifling. Instead she found herself stimulated anew, fascinated, half afraid that seven days in his company was far too long, yet would ultimately prove far too brief. Facing him, she felt alive in a way she'd never before known. Alive in far more than just the physical sense.

"No. Somehow I didn't expect you would lie."

"Am I confined to quarters?"

"What do you mean?"

"Times when you don't require my services—am I free to move about the gardens? I promise not to bolt."

"Feel free to enjoy the gardens at your leisure, Mr. Bridgeman. They're rather exceptional, if I do say so myself."

"Thank you. And Mr. Bridgeman was my father."

Fallon nodded. "The settee is quite comfortable. I'll have pillows and bedding sent over for you."

His gaze stopped her from leaving, almost as if he detained her physically. "Where will you sleep?"

"In my room, as I always do."

"Next to your husband?"

She paused for a moment, and twisted her wedding ring. "There is no longer a husband. He drowned. Is there anything further you require?"

"Only this."

Bridge spun her around so her spine was pressed flush against the door, his length meeting hers at every juncture, his sheer strength anchoring her in place. "I require this."

He tilted her head back, ripped the pins from her hair, then plunged his hands through the silken silver-blond veil, his fingertips urgent against her scalp as he licked her lips, readied them to receive his kiss.

"You can't possibly paint me if you don't know me in all the ways a woman knows a man."

His kiss was as strong and masterful as he was, possessing her, filling her completely. Hot and hungry, she felt herself being as helplessly devoured as the quail he'd picked clean earlier. Consumed. Emptied and refilled. There was mastery in the way he sucked the breath from her lips, then breathed for her when she forgot how.

He captured her hands, linked his fingers with hers, and pinned her arms out straight. One knee nudged her legs apart, making contact with that burning inner core, the pressure further inflaming her senses.

He pressed his pelvis against hers. She went up on tiptoe in an attempt to even out their heights, to feel the length of his erection where she needed it most. She rolled her hips from side to side, freed her hands and clawed his half-open shirt out of the way to touch his skin. To define each individually honed muscle. To commit him to memory. To paint him blindfolded if need be.

As her gropings grew more frantic his touch gentled, along with his kiss. Fallon melted. She trembled, weak and boneless and reliant upon him to support her, to hold her, to somehow extinguish the bonfire alight from within.

He seemed to know her better than she knew herself. Where she liked to be kissed, how she liked to be stroked. Nibbling, teasing, coaxing kisses turned needful as she kissed him back.

He broke the kiss. "What do you want?"

She hesitated.

"What do you want?" It was a question requiring an answer, and all the honesty she had demanded from him.

"You know. What you did before."

"Made you come? I watched you come. A woman transformed. A woman in rapture. You want that again?"

"Please."

"There are dozens of way to make a woman come. Hundreds, perhaps."

"I want to experience them all."

He smiled a satisfied smile, a cat with tail feathers in its mouth and cream dribbling from its whiskers. "I will do my best to see that you do."

"I need to paint you, as well."

"Greedy Fallon. Hungry for it all. I suspect you've been half starved your entire life." His words echoed through her with a ring of absolute truth. She *had* been half starved. Half alive. How had he seen? How had he known?

"And you?" She stroked his hardened length through his trousers, watched him close his eyes, savoring the pleasure of her touch. She grew bold. "Will you teach me the ways to make you come? To truly know you?"

"I'm yours to command." He swooped her up in his arms, crossed the room, and laid her gently upon the settee. She watched as he removed his shirt, revealing the planes and angles that she longed to paint and yearned to touch. "Are you quite certain you wouldn't rather paint me than fuck me?"

"It's too dark to paint."

"Yet never too light to make love." He had just started on his trousers, when there was a knock at the door.

Fallon started. "The servants. Your bedding."

"I'll attend to this." He readjusted his trousers and strode across the room, gloriously shirtless. She watched the movement of taut muscles in his shoulders and back, undulating ripples beneath a stretch of silken skin.

In the wink of an eye she skimmed off her underpinnings, swept them out of the way, and smoothed her skirt down primly. The moist heat between her thighs prickled and throbbed in the most eager of ways, impatient for his touch.

He dismissed the servants, dumped the pillows and bedding next to the settee, then knelt before her, darkly, boldly beautiful in the firelight.

"Do you always scream when you come?"

"Only the one time with you earlier."

"Are you quite sure?"

Considering that this afternoon was the first time she'd experienced such a phenomenon, she nodded.

"No one else has ever made you scream?"

"No one else has ever made me come."

"Never?" He sounded startled by her admission.

"I am, however, more than willing to have you remind me exactly what I've been missing."

"My pleasure." Deftly he grasped her stockings, unclasped them, and skimmed them down her legs, his touch as light as a butterfly wing against her skin. She felt a responding tightening low in her belly.

Deliberately he placed her bare foot on his crotch. The heat and hardness of his erection blazed from the sole of her bare foot up her leg and past the forbidden entrance to her inner secrets. "Oh, my," she said, flexing her foot slightly, rubbing it along the length and breadth of his swollen cock.

He captured her foot's mate, kissed the instep, followed by each toe, while his hand cupped her bare calf, moving in an insinuating up-and-down motion that mimicked the mating act. With each stroke his hand climbed higher, past her knee, almost but not quite to the juncture of her thighs. As the pressure of his touch increased, so did the pumping of her foot against his cock.

She was streaming wet, awash with needs she'd never before known, her senses heightened by the sensual way his day's shadowy growth of whiskers rasped against her bare leg as his questing lips made the journey upward. Leisurely he nipped and licked, the rampant sensations rendering her light-headed, near delirium.

He froze upon discovery of her pantiless state, then smiled up at her, wicked approval on his face.

"Mmmmm," he said, fingers spreading her slick outer lips, watching her pleasure at his touch. "You have a surprise or two of your own, I see."

"Perhaps I'm just getting to know you." She sucked in her breath as he brushed the swollen knot of her clitoris.

"You like that?"

"Mmmmmm." Head back, eyes aflutter with ecstasy, she squirmed against his fingers, seeking release.

He pushed her legs apart, opening her wider, making her aware of the cool air on her overheated, overstimulated flesh. "You have a beautiful pussy," he murmured. "Good enough to eat."

The stroking, intimate touch of his lips and his tongue sent a searing white heat through her. She panted and moaned as fresh waves of fire lapped over her.

"You're allowed to move, you know."

And move she did. Flexing her hips, she shifted with him, against him, affording him better access to her secrets. Every last one.

"You like that, I take it?" He was clever with his moves, pushing her to the brink, then withdrawing ever so slightly, leaving her breathless and begging for more, for the blessed release that he deliberately withheld.

"I find it a most exquisite form of torture," she said.

He glanced up at her from between her legs, his lips moist from her juices. "You taste delicious. Here." He teased her with his fingers inside her, then raised them to her lips. She opened her mouth obediently, unable to break his gaze. "Taste my fingers. Enjoy your sweetness."

Her hot, strong mouth pulled greedily on his appendages, first one, then two, then three, deeply, as if she would suck all of him until he was inside her.

Gently he freed his hand, rose, and unfastened his trousers. His huge cock sprang free, with a tiny tear of neglect weeping from its eye. She circled her lips with her tongue, mouth open, eager to taste him as he had tasted her.

"Open your blouse."

She did as she was bade.

"Free your breasts."

She yanked at her chemise, not caring if it ripped, fumbling with the laces until her breasts tumbled free, milky-white, the nipples rosy and flushed. He rubbed the tip of his engorged penis across each rosy crest, and they hardened instantly. Then he brought his cock to her month, circled the outline of her lips, teased her with his luscious, velvety tip. She tasted him, slightly salty-sweet, not unlike herself but different. His smell was musky and masculine and mysterious. She opened her mouth wider, as if to take him all in.

"Touch your breasts," he said. "Show me how they like to be touched."

Her breasts overflowed her hands, soft and voluptuous. She teased the nipples with flat palms, slowly at first, then faster, feeling a fresh outpouring of heat between her legs.

"Good," Bridge said. "And here's your reward." He slid his hot, hard cock between her lips slowly, a half inch, then withdrew it. She rubbed her breasts faster. This time he eased in the entire tip, allowed her tongue to circle it once before he withdrew it. Thus he continued, a little deeper, a little faster, in and out, careful not to give her too much at once. Not to let her suck too hard or too deep.

She whimpered in frustration, her eyes on his, pleading.

"Very well, my impatient one." He reached between her legs, separated the folds, and inserted two fingers inside her in perfect rhythm with his cock in her mouth—in, out, in, out.

When his thumb brushed her clitoris, something burst inside of her. Fallon convulsed. She screamed and screamed and screamed.

Bridge swore and pulled his cock from her mouth. He yanked her close and wrapped his arms around her tight, holding her until the spasms subsided.

"Did I hurt you?" she asked, when she could finally speak.

"What you did is nearly damage the ego of a man who prides himself on his control."

He pulled her to her feet, skinned out of his trousers, peeled off her disarrayed garments, and led her to the fire. "Now that we're done with the foreplay, I intend to fuck you silly."

Chapter Four

Bridge lowered Fallon to the rumpled bedding before the glowing embers of the fire he had lit earlier. Her breasts were luscious and full, her skin soft and creamy and touched with a surprising spatter of freckles. She looked thoroughly kissed, well loved, and ready for more, her lips swollen, her hair tumbled about her shoulders, her skin tinged pink and still slightly moist from her orgasm.

Bridge was no stranger to bedding beautiful women, but none had ever responded the way Fallon had, nearly causing him to lose his much-touted self-control. Just gazing upon her, he felt he might explode there and then. He took a breath and pressed his tongue to the roof of his mouth, a technique he'd found effective for controlling the inevitable, and then, with a groan of pleasure, he buried himself in her welcoming warmth.

He felt her muscles clench around him, the inner mouth of her so hot and tight, it took all of his control to withdraw, reenter, withdraw again.

She rocked her hips to match his rhythm. He grasped her bottom and raised her hips to accommodate him more fully. He was buried. Lost in her. Buried alive, unable to breathe, and he didn't even care.

He watched the flutter of her eyelids, the softening of her features signaling her pleasure. Pleasure that soon turned to urgency as she pumped faster, her nails raking his back, her breath coming in sexy pants. He felt the internal pressure build as her muscles tightened. He wanted to hold off, to watch her come again and again, to watch his shaft drive in and out of that delicious, slippery slit of hers.

But as he felt her start to come, his control shattered. Her vaginal muscles clenched and squeezed him tight. Semen shot from his cock with a force he'd never before experienced. He swallowed her scream and made it his own before he collapsed heavily atop her, sliding against her, both of them slick with perspiration. Even after it was over her muscles continued to milk him, squeezing out every last drop, greedily begging for more.

Beneath him, he felt her breathing gradually slow. Absently her fingers ruffled his hair and stroked his back. Bridge was amazed that he was not only allowing such attention but even enjoying it. He, who'd never been one to laze about after the sex act was finished, lay there savoring the shallow rise and fall of his partner's chest beneath his. The slow, steady beat of her heart. Or was that his? Could two hearts really beat as—

Damn!

He pushed himself to one elbow. Where had that thought come from? He was hardly some poetic bard or innocent youth in the first throes of infatuation, composing sonnets about his lady love. With an effort, he rolled off of Fallon and onto his feet. He added a log to the dying fire, the perfect excuse for him to get up. But why did he feel the need for an excuse? He never had in the past.

They came, he went, had been his creed. Yet, at the sight of Fallon lying there, all rumpled and delectable and sleepy, he just wanted to crawl back alongside her. To curl his body against hers like the petals of an unopened rose, to hold her close and watch the sexual contentment on her face soften into sleep.

The room felt cold once he was away from the warmth of her body, the heat of their passion, the tangled blankets.

"You have gooseflesh." She reached out a hand, a clear invitation to rejoin her, to snuggle against her and let the rest of the world go to hell.

"You're right." He reached for his trousers and stepped into them. He stabbed his arms through the sleeves of his shirt, once he found it beneath her frock.

"Where are you going?"

"Out for some fresh air."

"Are you coming back soon?"

He gave her a dispassionate look. "I don't know about you, but I'm far too old to be spending the night on a cold floor."

Her expression changed, grew guarded. She sat up, bedsheet modestly clutched across her breasts, and pushed the tangle of hair back from her face with an unsteady hand. The firelight traced her beauty, its light and shadows enhancing the purity of her bone structure. "I'll have a proper bed moved in here tomorrow."

"Hardly necessary. I'll only be here half a fortnight."

"Nonetheless, never let it be said that I'm an ungrateful hostess."

"Nor I a difficult . . . houseguest. Is that the correct term for my stay?"

She ignored his question as she rose gracefully to her feet, wrapping the linen sheet more securely about her. "Don't be up late. I plan to get an early start in the morning."

"An early start?" He was baiting her most deliberately.

"For our sitting," she said primly. "Your portrait." She managed to meet his gaze directly, despite her state of undress. "You were right about one thing. I can't wait to paint you—now that I'm better acquainted with the man beneath the flesh."

The studio door slammed behind Bridge's retreat and Fallon lowered herself to the settee with legs that still quivered. For years she had dreamed, wondered, fantasized about a physical encounter like the one she had just experienced. A sexual experience where she was lifted clean out of herself.

Where she lost herself, lost her entire identity, where everything disappeared save the connection she had with her partner.

She fumbled into her clothing, relieved to have some privacy in which to do so. She was not as easy with her nudity as Bridge clearly was. On the heels of her exhilaration came the realization that he was in her life for only seven more days.

And nights. Seven more nights.

Unless they were all like tonight. She had thought Bridge would choose to linger with her, to nest awhile in front of the fire. To share thoughts and feelings.

She laughed at herself. Men didn't share; they took what they wanted. If a woman got something in return, it was of little consequence to them.

Except Bridge gave. He'd been totally invested in her pleasure, possibly more so than his own.

Art, she reminded herself. Art was the most important thing.

The portrait, she would always have.

The man would never be hers.

BRIDGE HEARD the studio door open, saw Fallon's slender form silhouetted in the doorway, and ducked behind a bush as she walked to the house. He needed time alone. Time to think. Time to try to assess what exactly had happened back there with Fallon. What had suddenly changed so that he could have lain there forever, cocooned with her in a tangle of blankets and love?

He gave his head a shake as he walked back to the studio.

Perhaps he'd drunk too much wine. Not that he hadn't a hundred other times without the same result. Perhaps he was getting older. Maturing in his old age. His mother and his sisters would have quite the laugh about that. They had despaired of his ever being naught but the bratty younger brother, the one who was destined never to take life seriously. Until the day he had picked up a gun and gone off to fight.

He'd given up trying to gauge why he had been spared when other good men, men a damn sight better than he'd ever be, had fallen like flies. It was too much to understand.

He opened the studio door. Fallon's presence lingered in every corner; her scent wafted in the air. She'd gotten to him. He, who never allowed anything or anyone to affect him. He had to figure out a way to distance himself from her; he was there only long enough for her to paint him and to fuck him. Beyond that, nothing.

"YOU'RE RATHER CHEERFUL this morning, madam," remarked Mrs. Buttle, the plump, middle-aged housekeeper who'd been seeing to her comforts ever since Fallon's marriage to Captain Gilchrist. Indeed, they had mourned together and comforted each other through the loss from which Fallon had once thought she might never recover. Over time the sharp pain had subsided to a dull memory, ever present but no longer debilitating.

"I suspect it's the weather. More than a hint of summer, finally."

"A promise, to be sure."

"My houseguest, a young friend of Mrs. Stark, will be

staying in the studio a few days more. I will be working long hours, so please see that meals are delivered there on a regular basis." She paused, then added, "Quite sumptuous meals, for the food helps inspire me."

"Like last night?"

Last night's meal or last night's inspiration? "Exactly like last night. As I don't wish unnecessary disturbances, have the trays left outside the door. Foods that won't spoil if they're not immediately eaten."

"Yes, madam. Anything else?"

"Champagne. Lots of champagne. Strawberries. Buy them fresh at the market. Ghiradelli Chocolate. Fine cheeses."

Mrs. Buttle raised one brow but was too well trained to offer comment, for which Fallon was immeasurably relieved.

The dew lay heavily on the barely opened rosebuds and on the grass beneath her feet as she made her way at a deliberately slow pace from the house to the studio. Her skirt brushed against a laden peony bush and she felt the morning moisture on her hem, brushing against her ankles. The sensation naturally reminded her of Bridge. His mouth on her feet and ankles, before moving to possess her in a way no other man ever had. She embraced the memory, the feelings it evoked.

Was it only her perception, or did the sun shine a tad more brightly than days previous? Was the sky a more intense shade of blue, the scudding clouds a cleaner white in contrast? The air was positively redolent, heavy with the fragrance from the lush greens of her grounds.

No wonder she'd been unable to paint. Her senses had

been dulled, but were now gloriously brought back to life, thanks to Bridge. An artist of people, as he branded himself. She prayed her skills proved enough to do his likeness justice, that she could capture his true depth.

She pushed open the door and he turned, a little-boy petulance upon his face. "Tell your cook I detest oatmeal in the morning."

Fallon smiled. "Mrs. Buttle is Scots. She believes in the benefits of hearty rolled oats that stick to one's ribs and get one's day off to a proper start. What would you prefer?"

"Steak and eggs."

"Very well." She studied him in the unforgiving morning light. Remarkable, the beauty of such raw masculine power. "I'll see to it tomorrow. Now, we work."

He rose, liquid grace in his movements as he came her way. He allowed his fingertips to flutter ever so lightly against her throat. She forced herself to stand still, but swallowed thickly, and knew he felt the effect he was having upon her.

"Work, or allow ourselves to be inspired first?" he said in husky tones that chased magic tingles down her backbone, as if she were the xylophone and he the musician orchestrating her pleasurable response.

She stepped back, relieved when he didn't follow. "I long to paint you. I only hope I am able to do you justice."

He flashed a grin, incorrigible in its boyish complexities. "Will seven days serve long enough?"

Never. But Fallon refrained from giving voice to the traitorous thought. "It shall have to do."

"Same pose as yesterday?"

"If it pleases you."

"It would please me more to make you come. To see the sunlight play upon your skin. To taste the juices of your sex."

"It will be your skin exposed to the daylight, and yours alone," Fallon said in a tone she hoped brooked no argument. Could she even hope to resist, should he attempt to seduce her?

Her gaze fell to yesterday's charcoal sketches. They were some of her best work, yet to her critical eye, she knew she could do so much better. She glanced at her subject. He had discarded his shirt, and his back was toward her as he stepped out of his trousers. The curve of his spine was positively intoxicating, as was the long, lean line of muscle from gluteus maximus to splendidly formed hamstring. The man truly was poetry in motion, his skin dusted with dark curls in all the right places. She knew firsthand the soft texture of that skin where no hair grew. Knew its contrast, beneath her fingertips, with the springy dark thatch that ran from his breastbone to ring his navel, and plunge lower into the thick nest housing his splendid cock.

She sighed and forced herself to gaze upon him dispassionately as he arranged himself upon the settee.

"Wait. I need to drape the fabric."

Fallon reached around and above him, feeling the velvet slip through her fingers like water. She frowned. The velvet sucked up the light. She needed something different, a fabric to reflect the light. To reflect his splendor.

"It's no good," she said. "I need the satin."

"I can smell you," he said. "Your damp heat. I need to taste you. To bury my mouth against your clit, to lap at the special juices. Every woman tastes different. Did you know that?"

"How on earth would I have knowledge of such a thing?"

She located her bolt of satin, a blue so dark as to be nearly black. She tossed it atop the claret-colored velvet, appreciating the effect of one swathed atop the other. A study in contrasts, much as the man before her.

His cock swelled and hardened beneath her gaze. His eyes remained on hers as he licked his lips, as if recalling her special flavor.

"Do you want to know how you taste?"

"Not particularly," Fallon said. Though when she had tasted herself upon his fingers and his lips, she'd found it a positively heady potion. She positioned her easel before the settee and selected a blank, primed canvas from among her collection. At four feet in length and three feet in height, it was heavy, yet she was pleased when Bridge didn't offer his assistance. He'd settled himself atop the two swirled lengths of fabric. Sunlight spilled through the windows. Fallon selected her colors from the various tubes, squeezed them onto the palette, and began the painstaking task of mixing them to achieve exactly the right tone.

When she began to paint, her brush strokes were more sure than any she had ever before created. There was no hesitation, no faltering. She felt as if a special energy emanated from Bridge, through her, and onto the canvas. She trembled from the excitement of it, the sheer force of the energy.

Suddenly the unthinkable happened. She cast aside her brush in disgust. How unfair. Now, of all times.

Bridge raised one brow. "Are you finished with me so soon, then?"

"It's the unpredictable June weather." They both stared out the windows at the thick, gray blanket of cloud that obliterated the sun. "Just when things were going so well."

Bridge rose and stretched. "Am I to be allowed a viewing?"

"Not yet," Fallon said. "I've barely started."

"When?"

"Not until it's finished."

Thunder cracked through the sky. The glass window panes were pelted with thick, fat raindrops that ran in wild rivulets. She sighed, feeling her pent-up frustrations match the storm's mood.

"It won't last," Bridge said, as he strode about the studio, completely comfortable in his nudity.

Indeed, she was beginning to feel like the one who was incorrectly attired. Too many layers. The fire was ablaze, ensuring that Bridge didn't feel chilled. She mopped a trickle of perspiration from her forehead with her sleeve.

Bridge caught the action. "Too warm?"

She knew he'd suggest she remove a few layers. Or offer to do it for her.

"Not at all," she said in quick denial. Too quick, for he clearly wasn't fooled.

His eyes took on a mischievous glint. "I know how to cool you off."

He also knew how to get her totally overheated. On the

heels of her thoughts Fallon found herself halfway out the door, her hand caught firmly in his, before she realized his intentions.

"You are mad," she gasped as the summer rain hit her face. "You can't dance around my garden naked. What if someone sees?"

Her protests fell upon deaf ears as he caught her against him and swung her around. His steps were as correct as if they danced in a ballroom among hundreds, not dodged raindrops in the privacy of her studio garden amid the rain-drenched foliage and blooms.

"There's nothing like summer rain," Bridge said. "It's warm. Sensual."

He looked like a pagan god. His skin was slick and wet, as was his hair. He pushed it back off his forehead and raised his face to the sky. Fallon could feel the coolness of the rain penetrating her frock to her skin. Her nipples hardened beneath the damp fabric. The skirt held more weight as it clung to her legs. She should have been cool; instead she was inflamed by the sheer lustful sensuality of dancing in the rain with a beautiful, unclothed man.

Her sensual wantonness must have simmered over to him, for he slowed his steps and reeled her close. She could feel his hardened muscles at every juncture they met, his warm skin heating her through the dampened tangle of her frock.

"Tell me, Fallon. Have you ever made love in the rain?"

She could only shake her head in bewilderment, no longer feeling responsible for her actions or responses.

"I guarantee you, it's an experience like no other. One you will never forget."

She was ready for his kiss, eagerly welcoming the heady invasion of his tongue, the rough yet knowing pressure of his lips upon hers. The backs of his knuckles grazed her nipples, the barrier of wet cloth between her skin and his an enticement rather than a deterrent.

Fallon caught her breath as his lips abandoned hers to lavish attention on her throat and neck, her cheeks and eyelids. Raindrops fell upon her skin to mingle with the dampness of his kisses. He felt divine. Strong and sleek and slippery. She couldn't get enough of the rugged contours of his shoulders and back, his lean hips, the tight globes of his buttocks.

His cock was rigid against her belly and she knew the sudden urge to taste him as he had tasted her. She dropped to her knees before him and tentatively touched her dampened lips to the velvety softness of his tip, tasting a single salty drop of his semen. She heard him moan, the sound thundering through her and further inflaming her senses. Knowledge of the pleasure she could bring him was a new and intoxicating feeling.

She gripped his backside in the palms of her hands and slowly eased the entire head of his penis into her mouth. Tentatively at first, she circled it with her tongue. He buried his hands in her hair and clutched her scalp tightly. He didn't try to jam the entire length of his cock into her mouth the way her husband once had, making her gag and nearly vomit. Instead he murmured his approval as she continued to engulf his hardness in the satin heat of her mouth, inch my inch, sliding back when it became too much. She quickly realized he liked that and changed her tactics, sliding her round, hungry mouth up and down the hot swollen length of the underside of his shaft, sucking slightly, rewarded by another droplet of his creamy juices. He thrust his pelvis in time to her movements, intensifying the in-out motion.

She increased her speed accordingly, sucking harder, pulling him in deeper, until abruptly he pulled himself free.

She gazed up at him wide-eyed. "Did I do something wrong?"

He dropped to his knees alongside her. "You did something far too right, my love. But I'm not yet ready to have my release."

He ripped her underthings aside and pulled her, still kneeling, on top of him. The thick grass was tickly soft beneath her knees. He positioned himself so that he was able to lick the soft insides of her thighs. A rush of heat shot through her, a tremble of impatience that she knew he felt, for he laughed against her skin as he nibbled and tasted and licked near her mons.

When she shifted slightly to provide him better access, he shifted as well, holding her hips firmly in place. She stiffened slightly, feeling the new and slightly strange sensation of him licking her bottom. She heard his murmurs of approval as he gorged himself on first one cheek, then the other. Fallon closed her eyes and enjoyed the sensation. A new erogenous zone. A different trembling need. He spread the cheeks, accessing the deep crevice between, his hungry tongue loving and laving every inch of her. Desire built to unprecedented heights. She reached down and touched herself, only to feel him shift again, his lips replacing her tentative fingers.

He separated the folds of her lips and flicked his tongue against her clitoris, coaxing it from hiding.

Fallon caught her breath at the delicious ripples of pleasure flooding through her, a prelude of more to come.

"Touch your breasts," Bridge ordered. "Pinch your nipples through the dampness of your gown. Tell me how good it feels."

"Oh, yes." Fallon did as she was told, rewarded by that instant connection between her breasts and her womb, the heavy fullness intensifying and flooding her with fresh desire.

"Open the front of your dress."

Fallon's fingers trembled with impatience against the buttons but at last she succeeded, pulling her breasts free from the confines of her chemise, allowing their unbound splendor to drink up the softly falling rain.

"Beautiful," Bridge said. "Beautiful tits. A beautiful pussy."

He continued to feast hungrily between her legs while Fallon fondled her breasts and rubbed the wet, hard nubs of her nipples. He was tonguing her slit, in and out, his tongue working like a tiny darting penis. He teased her inner lips, dampening his fingers, then found the tiny tight bud of her anus. Slowly he rubbed, and Fallon felt it unfolding beneath the pressure, opening to the questing pressure of his little finger. With his finger working her rear and his tongue inside her honey pot, Fallon abruptly experienced the most intense orgasm ever, hot, fast wave after wave of wonderment such as she had never known. His clever fingers replaced his tongue on her clit, with just enough pressure to coax out every last throbbing ripple of pleasure. Then he simply cupped her womanhood tightly while the sensations subsided.

Chapter Five

"*Oh.*" Fallon could barely speak, let alone move. Hugging her tightly against him, Bridge shifted them both to new positions. Now she reclined upon the bed of soft grass and he knelt above her, his form sheltering her from the gentle mist-like rain that enshrouded them and lent an air of surrealism to their encounter.

The sexy scent of Fallon was enhanced by the rich, pungent odor of damp earth and rain-kissed fauna. The only sound beyond their breathing was the steady light rain landing upon wide-leafed foliage and waterlogged flower heads.

From his new vantage point Bridge gazed down at Fallon. Her frock had burst open to display her voluptuous milk-white breasts. He cupped them, noting how rugged his hands looked against her creamy skin, glistening with a rain-kissed sheen.

He ducked his head and tongued her nipples lightly at first, before pulling them deep inside the cavern of his mouth. He felt the hard, cold buds respond to the heat of his mouth as a flower responds to the sun.

Dampening the divide between her breasts with his tongue, he pushed their scrumptious softness together, cupped them in his palms, and eased his aching cock into the snug sheath. She was moist and warm and slippery and he nearly lost it, hearing her tiny gasp of surprise.

"Has no one fucked you in the tits before?"

His thumbs teased her nipples, enjoying their response. The areolas, the color of softly drying red rose petals, pulled tight and hard as he rolled the pads of his thumbs across each bud.

"Never." She raised her head to answer and his cock grazed the pink softness of her lips. He didn't know where she got the idea from, but suddenly Fallon stuck out her tongue and tickled the tip of his cock as he thrust forward between her breasts, hot and hard and so ready to explode he had to grit his teeth.

"Does that hurt?" She thought his expression was more pain than pleasure.

"God, no. Push your breasts together tightly for me."

She did as he bade her, taking over the pressure of his

hands cupped around her breasts, leaving him free to touch her everywhere. Wet hair, soft cheeks, swanlike neck, and smooth shoulders all clamored for his attention as he continued to pump away at her tits, loving the way she took him in, her darting pink tongue no longer shy about teasing and licking his cock every chance she got.

He could feel himself nearing the end of his control. Reaching back between her legs, he probed the slick folds of her womanhood. She was so hot and so wet, and so ready to come again, that he barely grazed her labia lips, hardly even teased her clitoris, to feel her sudden gush of pleasure.

His body responded with release so intense that he reared up, and watched his semen spurt forever across her, mixing with the raindrops and the scent of their lust.

She held him tightly within the glove of her breasts, rubbing him in a gentle, loving way, as she milked every last droplet of his juices. Bridge leaned forward and pushed the damp tangle of hair back from her face, enjoying the look of intense rapture he saw there. He adored pleasuring women, yet never before had a woman taken so much and given so much in return.

"Let's get you inside and dried off." He tugged the folds of her gown together, mopping at the sticky residue of their love, before he helped her to her feet.

"I'm not certain I can stand," Fallon said in a shaky voice.

Bridge scooped her up in his arms and carried her over the threshold of the studio. The outbuilding he had at first considered his prison had suddenly become a haven, a place where the outside world could never intrude. He slammed the door behind him and resisted the urge to lock it in an attempt to keep the rest of the world at bay, even as he knew a week spent exploring each other meant that their worlds would never be the same afterward.

He set her on her feet before the fire. "Can you stand now?"

She nodded shakily and pulled the folds of her dress across herself, trying ineffectually to smooth the grass-stained wrinkles of her skirt.

Bridge ripped impatiently at the bedclothes he'd dropped off the settee earlier, draping one blanket around himself and carrying a second one to Fallon.

"You've got to get out of this wet gown."

She gazed up at him, the firelight reflecting confusion in her eyes. "Bridge, what just happened?"

"What do you mean?" With one corner of the blanket he mopped at his damp hair, slicking it straight back from the broad planes of his forehead. "We fucked in the rain. Which served to heighten the sensations, finding oneself one with nature and all that. Primitive, basic rutting. You must admit, it was mighty fine."

"Mighty fine," Fallon echoed, her voice quivering with uncertainty.

Bridge busied himself fetching another piece of firewood to add to the fire. Fine fucking aside, it would never do for her to realize that he was every bit as awed by the sheer power and magic of their coupling as she was.

While he stoked the fire, Fallon made her way to the window. The sky was lightening, the rain had nearly let up. As she watched, a bright swath of color arched across the sky. The brightest, most intense rainbow she had ever seen shimmered, then doubled, cocky with its power and ability to reflect and admire its own splendor. It reminded her of Bridge. For he, too, was cocky with his power and abilities.

"A double rainbow," Bridge murmured directly in her ear. "Considered by some to be good luck. Double the pots of gold and such."

Fallon hadn't heard him come up directly behind her, and she half turned, close enough to touch, to burrow against him. To smell his distinctive masculine scent, damp earth and raw sex.

Before she knew what she was doing, she stepped into the circle of his arms, kissed his naked chest, and nuzzled his neck, as his arms opened and enfolded her. Pulling her tight, he held her secure, safe from the outside world and unwanted intrusions.

"Why am I always the one who is naked, while you continue to be clad in entirely too many clothes?" Bridge asked.

"I own you," Fallon said. "It's the slave—master role."

"What do you think would happen," Bridge asked, serious for once, "if I were to own you?"

Fallon glanced away, afraid her face might mirror her feelings. Afraid that, in one way, he already did own her.

She touched his breastbone with her index finger. "You, good sir, would be a most formidable master. Relentless. Demanding. Uncompromising. I fear for the poor maiden who is unlucky enough to find herself enslaved to you."

"And would you be my willing subject?"

"Never!" Fallon smiled.

Always, she thought. She was so enamored of Bridge, she was likely to do anything he bade. Witness how many times she'd had him and even now, temporarily sated, her traitorous body clamored for more. God help her, yes—she would do almost anything to have him again.

"I think," Bridge said with a sly smile, "if there was an auction, I should bid on you."

Fallon couldn't help but lick her lips at the prospect. Couldn't put paid to her insatiable curiosity. "And then?"

"Ah." Bridge's fingers probed the soft, vulnerable curves of her shoulders and neck. She moved against him like a cat begging to be petted. "What would I have my lady Fallon do? Pose for me hours on end, stiff and cold? Unlikely. I believe I would have you trained as my own personal geisha. Trained to do nothing but serve and pleasure me."

"Serve you how?" Fallon asked.

"Prepare my bath. Bring my meals. Pour my wine. See to my every creature comfort."

"A housemaid," Fallon said. "How very unoriginal. I believe I'll go and change into something dry, and see if dinner is on its way."

"Are you aware of the way you resort to flight whenever something makes you uncomfortable?"

Fight or flight, Fallon thought. She could never fight him. "Don't be silly. I'm hungry, is all."

"You definitely have succeeded in stimulating my appetite," Bridge said, his hands resting with heavy possessiveness on her shoulders in such a way that his body heat seared through her damp frock. "Yet I fear it will not be satisfied by mere food and drink."

Fallon shuddered at the raw carnality. Everything about Bridge, from his stance to the intensity of his gaze, promised sex and more sex. And lord help her, she wanted all he had to offer, even as she knew she would only be left wanting more.

She turned away. What she desired from him was not something he had to give. She must content herself with capturing him on canvas, holding on to some small part of him forever, along with the memories of this time. She draped her wrap across her shoulders.

"Don't be long," Bridge said.

"I thought you were mine to command, not give the orders."

He shrugged carelessly. "I don't manage subservience terribly well. Besides, I miss you when we're parted."

There was a wistfulness in his words and his tone that almost convinced Fallon of his sincerity as she ran quickly back to the manor house. Was there a chance he meant what he said? That he longed for her company as she longed for his? The man was a master manipulator, she reminded herself. No doubt every woman who found herself on the receiving end of his amour believed herself more special, more important, than any who had gone before.

She was brought smartly back to earth by Mrs. Buttle's goggle-eyed viewing of her bedraggled appearance.

"You've nigh gone and destroyed a perfectly good gown, madam."

"Too true, Mrs. Buttle. I slipped on the mud in the wet

grass. Mind you watch your own step if you venture out. Or better yet, stay indoors while it storms."

"Yes, madam. I be having no reason to leave the house."

Fallon stiffened. Was that censure in the woman's tone? Or was she being overly sensitive? "It's been a long time since we've had guests," she said smoothly.

"Certainly, madam. The meal trays are ready. Would you have me send them over?" Her housekeeper continued to avoid her eye. *She can't know what I've been doing with Bridge,* Fallon thought guiltily. *Why is she acting so odd?*

"Yes, please. I shall change into something dry and be along straight away."

"Will you be needing a hand getting changed, then?"

"Mrs. Buttle. Never before have I required a hand to get changed. Why would you suddenly think things to be different?"

"Seems changes going on, is all."

"I'm painting again. And very happy about it. Which is the only change you need concern yourself with."

Upstairs in her room, Fallon peeled away her ruined clothing and perused herself critically in the cheval looking glass. Small wonder Mrs. Buttle seemed disapproving. She was more than just a little rumpled. Her cheeks were pink, and although she could attribute their high color to the warmth inside after the coolness of the rain, she knew it was much more than that. She looked happy. Well kissed and thoroughly loved, with her hair spilled in tumbled disarray about her shoulders.

She cupped her breasts in her hands and pushed them

together. Memory of the way Bridge had slid his hot, hard cock between them and taken his pleasure, while still giving her hers, sent a fresh hot wave of longing thundering through her loins. What on earth was happening? When had she become so wanton? If he was here right now, she could quite happily tumble him again. But when would his portrait get painted if they spent all their time in carnal pursuits?

Surely, she thought as she selected a clean and pressed frock, one of a rosy hue that matched the color in her cheeks and enhanced the brightness of her eyes, surely they could find time to do both. Time for detached physical pleasure and enjoyment of each other's company.

She was not allowed to get attached to Bridge, she told herself with new firmness. For hadn't she learned to get through life by allowing herself to care in only the most shallow of fashions? Anna was the one exception, the one person who had pushed aside her reticence. Who understood her fears and where they came from. Caring too much ultimately hurt too much.

It had begun with her parents' death, leaving her to be raised by a strict, unemotional aunt and uncle. Then there was her tiny infant, whose loss she still felt when she allowed herself the memory. Most recently, the Captain had been taken from her side. She pulled on her clean frock and tidied her hair. At least with Bridge, she knew from the outset that he would disappear from her life shortly. She could be prepared.

Fallon sensed something different the moment she entered the studio. Bridge had set their meal out on the table as he had the day before, but he was fully dressed, including his jacket and cravat. His white shirt appeared crisply immaculate. His boots gleamed. His trousers sheathed his splendid legs in such a way as to be almost indecent. Just the sight of those powerful limbs was enough to melt her insides. How well she knew those strong, capable hands and the wonders of their touch.

"I didn't know we were to dine formally," she said, her hands fluttering near her throat. Suddenly she didn't know what to do or where to look. The sight of Bridge, clothes or no, sparked a dangerous hunger.

"I've decided to call off our arrangement," he said with the utmost casualness.

Fallon felt as if her stomach hit her knees with a hollow thud of disappointment.

"I mean to return to Boston immediately."

"It's too late to renege," she said with unusual force. "Anna paid for your services for one full week."

"A wrong I intend to put right."

Her gaze followed his to the table, where a significant pile of bills lay. "I don't want your money. And neither does Anna."

"Consider it my bequest to a worthy cause, in the manner you first suggested. A far more noble gesture than my week-long offer of services."

Fallon picked up the bills and thrust them into his uncooperative hand. They fluttered to the floor between them. "You entered into an agreement. Your portrait is only half done. Now, enjoy your meal and remove your clothing. I quite fancy the light at this moment."

"Be careful, Fallon."

"Careful of what?"

"Be careful that you know what you want. Along with exactly what you are getting."

"I want to finish painting you," Fallon said.

"So you maintain." Bridge poured himself a glass of champagne from the open bottle and took a sip. "Very nice," he said. "French."

"Of course. My husband sailed the world. He had very good taste in wine."

"And in women," Bridge said, tilting his glass in her direction, toasting her beauty. He picked up a fresh strawberry from the bowl and took a bite.

"I didn't really want to leave, you know. I'm quite enjoying myself here."

"So why the charade?" Fallon picked up a toast round topped with foie gras.

"I wanted to ensure that you are as committed to the project as I am."

"I told you, I have every intention of seeing the portrait completed."

"I'm not talking about the portrait," Bridge said.

"I fear we're at cross-purposes. What else is there?"

"I refer to us, Fallon. The way in which we are getting to know each other inside out. The secrets we may have to give up. The baring of our souls, along with our bodies."

"Really, Bridge, I . . ."

He watched the way her hands fluttered like a defenseless bird caught in a trap. "It's quicksand, Fallon. And if I step into it, I take you with me. You have my word."

"Ah. So you were trying to spare me, is that it?"

"No, my dear. I was trying to spare us both. But I fear it is far too late for that. Now I have new inspiration for your artist's soul."

He rose and went around behind her, where he began to unfasten the back of her dress.

"Bridge, I . . ."

He felt her tremble at his touch. Her nape looked delicious. He fastened his lips against it and felt her shuddering response. Her muscles softened like warm wax, her body pliant within his touch.

She was his.

She might think she owned him, that he was hers to command. In reality, the opposite was true. And they both knew it.

He peeled off her clothing, piece by piece. It was high time he remained clothed while her naked splendor was exposed to his admiring eye.

"You're beautiful," he said, his hands reverently tracing her feminine curves and valleys as she reclined on the settee.

He plucked a large, ripe strawberry from the bowl, took a bite, then pressed it to her lips. She took a tiny nibble, her eyes on his, unsure what would follow.

How delightful she was. Such a heady mixture of virtue and seduction.

The half-eaten berry trailed its juice across her chest as he traced the shape of her breasts, then colored her nipples the deep dark red of the berries. He licked them clean, then started again.

"Oh, look," he said happily. "Whipped cream. Dear Mrs. Buttle. A woman after my own heart."

"I doubt this was what she intended," Fallon said as he dipped his fingers in the bowl of thick cream and dotted them atop her red, cherrylike nipples.

"I need more." He scooped a handful of cream onto her breasts like snow-topped mountain peaks, then topped each one with a strawberry.

"So," she said huskily. "How do I taste?"

"I'm about to find out." He took another scoop of cream and spread it over her mons. She shifted, allowing him easier access.

"You're so hot," he said. "The cream is starting to melt."

"You're sure it's not the fire?"

"I am very certain it's you."

He kept one hand on her pubes, teasing and torturing her inner lips while he nibbled at the strawberries and cream cresting her breasts, one at a time.

She was moving with him, rolling her hips, begging for more, rubbing her tight hot little box against his hand like a wanton feline. He obliged with more pressure in just the right place, and at the same time he lightly nipped her with his teeth. He was careful not to bite, only to graze the sensitive area as he continued to lap at the remainders of his creamy feast.

He felt the catch in her breathing as her orgasm started to build. He fed it to her bit by bit, rubbing, slowing, rubbing harder, biting, licking, sucking. Then she came, with a deep, keening moan that reverberated into him, racing through his veins like hungry brush fire.

"God, Fallon. Do that again."

He knelt before her, smeared her sex with more cream, and fell upon her like a parched desert traveler coming upon an oasis.

No gentleness, no teasing now. Just raw, primitive hunger and a thirst that only Fallon could quench. Her juices sweetened the richness of the cream, turned it into ambrosia. He could eat her forever; exist on nothing save Fallon. Exist in a world that contained only her. Their own Eden. For she was beauty and strength. She was him and he was her.

Quicksand, he had told her. He was going down without a struggle; he had no desire to fight his way free.

He became aware of her trying to push him away.

"No more," she panted. "I can't possibly . . ."

"Of course you can."

And he proceeded to prove, over and over again, that she could.

FALLON DOZED BRIEFLY, and woke ravenous. Bridge sat staring out the window, still fully dressed. She wondered if he was still considering leaving.

He must have heard her stir, for he turned. "I heated some water over the fire so you could wash."

"That was thoughtful."

She watched as he tipped water from the pot into a bowl, tested it for temperature, dipped a flannel into it. She reached for the cloth.

"Allow me," he said. And with economical motions he removed all residue of the sticky creaminess, along with all residue of his possession. She wondered if his actions were in any way symbolic.

"I'm starved," she said, reaching for a chunk of cheese and a slice of bread. "Did I sleep long?"

"Just long enough for the light to become absolute perfection."

As Bridge disrobed, she dressed. And just like that, they returned to their former roles. Bridge resumed his pose on the settee while Fallon donned her smock and took up her paints and brushes, just in time to be interrupted by a discreet knock at the studio door.

Chapter Six

She used the time it took to reach the door to compose herself. Her houseman, Franklin, stood just outside and she swallowed the sensation of alarm, knowing he wouldn't dream of interrupting her on a whim.

"Franklin, what is it? Is something wrong?"

The man was a dear, but he had a problem with stammering and now proved no exception. Fallon forced herself to be patient as he floundered.

"B-b-begging yer p-pardon, misssus, b-but the Captain Mum has just now arrived."

"The Captain Mum." Dear Lord, her mother-in-law.

What timing! Fallon pulled her thoughts together frantically while poor Franklin stood wringing his hands together. "How does she seem?"

"P-p-pardon?"

"She's bound to be tired after her journey. Have Mrs. Buttle prepare her room and fix her a tea tray. Please inform her I'm working in my studio and shall see her after she is rested."

"V-very *gooood,* missus."

She shut the door behind the man and turned to Bridge, who was watching her with unabashed interest.

"Just who, pray tell, is the Captain Mum?"

"My late husband's mother. She's rather demanding, at best. Quite in her second childhood."

"Some of us, on the other hand, never quite leave our first."

"So I've noticed." Fallon resumed her spot at the easel. Bridge was right: the lighting was nothing short of perfection. As was her subject. There was no sound in the studio save that of their breathing and the soft swish of sable bristles against the canvas.

Fallon felt remarkably uplifted. Her work had reached a new, higher dimension and so had she. All due to Bridge.

As a model, he was an inspiring subject. The light loved him, dancing along his skin, emphasizing the contours of his rugged muscular torso, his strong legs and shoulders. And his hands. How she loved his hands. As she concentrated on painting them, on detailing each knuckle, she recalled the way those hands made her feel; the erogenous zones that sprang to life beneath those talented fingers.

She felt herself flush and tingle at the memory. The bowl of whipped cream caught her eye. She could so easily put aside her brush, scoop up a handful of cream, mound it onto Bridge's cock, and eat him the way he had eaten her.

Her breath snagged. A trickle of perspiration ran from her hairline to her brow and she wiped it away impatiently with the sleeve of her smock.

"Are you warm?" Bridge inquired.

No detail ever escaped his notice. "A little," she said.

"Perhaps you ought to slow down. You've been working extremely hard."

"I'm afraid you might leave while the portrait is only half done. You seem anxious to be on your way."

"Rest your mind, Fallon. It was only a test to see if you are as committed to our arrangement as I am."

"I never start a project and not see it through to completion."

"Good," he said easily. "And neither do I."

His words gave her pause. Could she pretend not to be finished? Would he delay his departure at her request? No, they both knew that the sooner they got through this, the sooner his obligation ended, leaving him free to go. Fallon ignored the inner pang she felt. For here and now, he was hers. There was no point in ruining what little time they had with needless fretting.

She forced her entire concentration on her creation. When had her hands, her eye, become so sure? Had this talent inside her simply been sleeping? Awaiting a kiss from Bridge's talented lips to bring it to life? What if it became like Samson's strength, and her talent left her at the same time as Bridge? What if her skill proved only as good as her subject, with lifeless subjects equating lifeless skill. What if it was Bridge himself, his energy, that was solely responsible for this newfound rush of creative genius? For without a doubt, this portrait would be the best work she had ever done.

"There." At long last Fallon laid her brush aside and arched her neck, stretching her head from side to side and rolling her aching shoulders.

Bridge rose gracefully, with no hint in his movements that he must feel more cramped than she, after holding his pose for hours.

"May I see?" He started to pad barefoot toward her. In the room's fading light, the beautiful yet neutral subject of her work somehow took on an entirely different persona. Man. Raw. Primitive. Sexual.

"Not till it's done. A superstition of mine." Fallon rounded the easel, fumbling with the ties of her smock. Bridge pushed her hands away and unfastened the ties. Before she knew how it happened, his hands were everywhere, strong fingers and knuckles kneading the knotted muscles in her neck and shoulders.

"Oh . . ." She groaned at the pleasure wrought by his touch.

"I'll rub your back if you'll rub mine," Bridge said suggestively. The husky timbre of his voice, coupled with his nearness, garnered the expected response. She felt herself draw closer, her fingers itching to touch the sleek lines of his back, to make him feel every bit as good as he was making her feel.

"Is that a fair exchange?" she asked.

"I would say so."

"But you're stronger. I'll gain the most benefit."

"I'll be the judge of that." He started to unfasten her frock.

"You have this penchant for seeing me disrobed at the slightest whim."

"A man can hardly be faulted for longing to admire, to touch, to taste your soft skin."

"A quick backrub only. Then I must see to my guest."

"I thought I was your most important guest, whose needs required seeing to on a regular basis."

"As you take every opportunity to remind me," she remarked dryly as she slipped from her garments, wrapped herself in a sheet, and lay facedown upon the settee.

The satin and velvet beneath her was still warm from Bridge's body. It felt sinfully sleek and soft beneath her. Small wonder he didn't seem to mind posing there, doubtless dreaming up new and delicious ways to pleasure her while she worked away.

She felt him straddle her, one knee on either side of her hips. She caught a vague whiff of some new fragrance, a mysterious spicy floral concoction, before she felt his oil-slick hands smooth the planes of her back.

She attempted to lever herself up and around. "What's that?"

Bridge urged her shoulders back down flat. "It's a special oil I picked up in my travels."

"It smells very exotic."

"It's credited with stimulating and relaxing the subject at the same time."

"That's quite the contradiction," she said, sinking into the settee as his hands moved surely across her shoulders, probed the tender places of her neck, then smoothed their way down her spine, pulling and pushing and kneading in all the right spots. "I do believe you're as much a contradiction as that oil you have," Fallon murmured sleepily. "You're very good at this, by the way."

"I told you before, I'm an artist of people. Few people realize the true importance of the sense of touch. Of skin against skin. It's an infant's first memory, one which lingers with us our entire life. People who live with a lack of touch grow ornery and moody and have no idea of the reason for their crotchetiness."

"I never thought of it that way," Fallon said. But it was true. Her parents had died, and her aunt and uncle were not at all touching people. Perhaps the constant stirring of dissatisfaction she'd felt with her life could all be harkened back to that.

"I come to life beneath your touch," she said impulsively, then immediately wished she could take back her words.

He laughed, his hands finding and relaxing the tensed knots of muscle. "Touch need not be sexual to be effective."

But all of his touch had a sensual feel. The way his hands sleeked her back and spine, traced her shape, lingered over her waist and hips, then found their way to the rounded cheeks of her bottom.

She let out a deep, contented sigh. How could she fail to

feel sexual when Bridge was touching her thus? He shimmied lower and she felt his lips replace his hands on her derriere, kissing and tonguing and licking her there.

She shifted slightly, signaling her pleasure as he continued his attentions. His tongue moved in whirling circles across her skin, up her back, then settled on the back of her neck.

"More relaxed now?" he murmured, stretching his naked length atop her.

"Mmmmmm," Fallon murmured. "I'm afraid I shall not give half so good a back rub to you. I've not had the practice."

"You have yet to disappoint me."

She felt him playing with the soft wisps of hair against the back of her neck, twining them around his fingers. "I'm glad. Let's see what type of back rub I can manage."

They traded positions, with Fallon straddling Bridge.

She reached for the exotic oil he had left within reach, poured a small measure into the palm of one hand, rubbed her hands together, then swished them across the planes of Bridge's back.

"I love your musculature," she said. He was lean yet sinewy, the muscles slack as he relaxed, yet she knew the awesome strength he wielded. "But I don't feel very confident about what I'm doing." She had no concept of any particular area that might require more pressure or special attention, the way he had intuitively known with her.

"You're doing fine."

She didn't want to do "fine"; she wanted to surprise him. She wanted to seduce him. She wanted him to crave her the way she constantly craved him.

She bent over him and breathed hotly against the back of his neck before pressing a line of kisses there. Then slowly she let her breasts replace her hands on his back, rubbed them lovingly up and down the length of his spine, and across the blades of his shoulders, glorying in her power.

She heard him groan and continued her assault upon his senses. Her nipples budded against his skin, begging for more. She felt herself grow wet, her mons riding the globes of his behind—her legs spread apart, all of her pressed wantonly against all of him.

"Fallon," he said huskily. "You have an unfair advantage over me."

"One I fully intend to exploit," she replied, rubbing against him, loving that he was pinned beneath her, helpless to touch her, powerless to do anything other than enjoy the sensations.

She wriggled lower so that she could drag her breasts across his backside. He raised it slightly, and she recalled how it had felt when he kissed her there.

She reached between his legs and positioned his hard cock so she could rub his rear and cock and balls. He groaned deeply, widened his legs to allow her better access. Leaning forward, she kissed him, tentatively at first, then with growing enthusiasm at his response.

She couldn't get enough of him, kiss him enough, everywhere. As she tongued his buttocks and rubbed his balls, his excitement was contagious, rendering her hot and wet, focused solely on him. She dipped her pinkie finger into the jar of oil, then slid it daintily into his anus the way he had with her. He nearly rose off the settee with a groan of pleasure as she settled beneath his legs and licked his cock and balls with lusty enthusiasm, while she continued to slide her finger in and out of him. When he tried to stop her, she persisted. She had him helpless, the way he'd had her.

The power she felt, as he came!

Fallon realized that the mere sex act itself involved mostly taking pleasure from one's partner. The act of making love, on the other hand, highlighted one's partner's pleasure over one's own. A truly glorious experience!

Bridge rolled over and attempted to pull her up atop him. "Your turn," he said huskily.

"I think not," Fallon said, still high on the power of her newfound skills. Why on earth would she surrender that power? Lie writing and helpless beneath him, desperate for something only he could give her, when it was far more empowering to remain as she was, to savor the heightened sense of arousal stemming from the pleasure she'd granted him?

She evaded his grasp and slid quickly back into her clothing. "Unfortunately," she said, "it'll have to wait. I've neglected my houseguest long enough."

She left the studio and passed through the kitchen, pausing to praise Mrs. Buttle and cook for the meal preparations that she saw under way.

"Captain Mum had a hearty tea tray and a lie down. She's just come down to the drawing room, madam."

"Did she seem miffed that I didn't greet her personally?"

"Franklin and I explained that you were busy with a commission and had to work while the light was right. She didn't make no mind that I saw."

"Thank you, Mrs. Buttle. I knew I could count on you."

She found her mother-in-law in the drawing room, flipping through the pages of a book of landscape paintings by Claude Joseph Vernet. "Eloise, my dearest, please forgive my shameful neglect of you. How long will you stay?"

"Just the night, Fallon. I'm traveling through to meet friends on the Cape. And I must apologize for dropping in unannounced, but you once said I was always to feel a part of this household."

"I meant it most sincerely."

Eloise was a tiny bird of a woman with bright eyes, smooth skin and fluffy blond hair, which, although unnatural on a woman of her years, she somehow managed to pull off. Perhaps due to her little-girl mannerisms.

"It's a relief to see you looking so in-the-pink, my dear. Rumors do fly through the city."

"What sort of rumors?" Fallon asked, her immediate thoughts on Bridge and his presence at her estate.

"Oh, you know—that you're depressed, or secretly drinking out here, unable to contain your grief. That sort of thing. You have been reclusive."

"As you can see for yourself, I am quite well and sober to boot." Fallon laughed.

"And painting again, Mrs. Buttle tells me, which is surely good news. I hear you have a resident model."

"A young friend of Anna's has commissioned me to paint him," Fallon said. "It's challenging work, but very rewarding."

Eloise blinked girlishly. "I can't wait to meet this young friend of Anna's. He'll join us for dinner?"

"Oh no, he's, uh . . . he's much too shy."

"Nonsense," Eloise said. "He shall join us if I must go over there and fetch him myself. I always enjoy the stimulation of a young person's perspective. Most enlightening and thought-provoking."

"I hardly feel that—"

"Fallon, dear." The innocent sparrow turned into a hawk, predatory and dangerous. "My mind is made up. Surely you have no reason *not* to invite him to our table?"

Did she read a veiled threat in those smoothly modulated words?

"Of course not. I'll fetch him myself before the meal. Now, do tell me what gossip I've missed in town."

Since gossip was Eloise's specialty, Fallon settled back, pasted a smile on her face, and tried to devise a way to avoid having Bridge and Eloise meet. In the end, she decided there was nothing for it but to warn Bridge to be on his best behavior. Both their reputations were at stake, and even if he cared naught for his own, she hoped he had a care for hers.

She said as much to him, once Eloise had run dry of her stories and entreated Fallon to "fetch the dear boy to join us."

"Fallon, my sweet," Bridge crooned. "I adore little old ladies. I shall have the Captain Mum eating out of my hand in no time."

"I beg you, don't volunteer any information. Be polite, yet distant."

"You mean," Bridge murmured suggestively, "I'm not to tell her just how you scream when I make you come?"

"You are incorrigible!" Fallon turned away to hide her slight flush of excitement at his words. Just the memory of their lingering pleasures had her limbs aquiver, and a rush of moist heat seeping between her legs.

"Come along," Fallon said. "She's waiting."

Eloise was seated before the fire, sipping a sherry. At the doorway to the drawing room, Bridge came to an abrupt halt and snatched Fallon with him around the corner, out of sight and earshot. "That's your mother-in-law?"

"Come along, Bridge. She's hardly that formidable-looking."

"Worse yet," Bridge said. "She's the one who lost in the bidding against your friend Anna."

Fallon felt her eyes widen in amazement. "Surely you jest?"

"Afraid not."

"Surely Anna would have said something, would have warned me."

"I doubt she knew who her most vigorous opponent was. I had a clear view of the entire assemblage."

"This is a disaster," Fallon murmured.

"I do recall being somewhat relieved when she finally dropped out of the bidding, leaving the way clear for your friend." He started forward.

Fallon grabbed his arm to detain him. "You can't go in there now. She'll know!"

"Ah, but she'll also know that *I* know. And she's hardly interested in jeopardizing her own position; trust me. I'm only here to have you paint me, nothing more. For all she knows, I still owe my week of servitude to your friend."

Fallon straightened her spine along with her fortitude, already longing for the meal's end and the evening to be behind her.

"Eloise, darling. It was difficult to persuade him to join us, but here is Anna's young friend, Montague Bridgeman. Mr. Bridgeman, may I present my mother-in-law, Mrs. Edward Gilchrist."

"A pleasure, madam." Bridge bowed low over the older woman's hand. "May I say what a delightful surprise it is to find myself dining with two beautiful women. I fear after a day spent in each other's company, Mrs. Gilchrist and I both normally seek our solitude."

Fallon had to hand it to her mother-in-law. Not a flicker of recognition crossed the older woman's face, nor did any speculative glances come her way. Perhaps, as Bridge had said, it would be just fine.

"The portrait is for you, young man?"

"A surprise for my fiancée. I beg you to keep your council."

"Certainly." She arched a questioning look in Fallon's direction. "Might I sneak a quick peek in the morning, my dear?"

"You know I never allow anyone to see an incomplete work."

"That's true," Bridge said. "Even I am not allowed the teensiest preview."

They were saved from further chitchat by the bell announcing dinner. Bridge, at his most gracious, offered each woman an arm to escort them to the table.

Fallon watched approvingly as he pulled out Eloise's chair and saw her comfortably settled. Mrs. Buttle had outdone herself. The linen was flawless, enhanced by fresh flowers and candles, gleaming cutlery, and the best gold-rimmed china.

Eloise nodded her approval at their surroundings. "I'm happy to see the room being used as it was intended, my dear. The Captain would most certainly approve. You always were such a gifted hostess."

"Mrs. Gilchrist has been making me feel most comfortable here, as well," Bridge said smoothly, grinning at her rakishly across the table. Fallon started when she felt the pressure upon her ankle beneath the table. Surely that was no accident, the positioning of Bridge's foot against hers? A quick glance his way assured her it was not.

She barely recovered in time to signal Mrs. Buttle to begin serving the soup from the silver tureen.

"You said your portrait is a surprise for your fiancée, Mr. Bridgeman?" Eloise asked as she sipped daintily at her seafood chowder. "When are the upcoming nuptials planned?"

"We have set no firm date yet," Bridge said. "She's off touring Europe first."

"How bold," Eloise remarked.

No bolder than Bridge, Fallon thought crossly. How had he taken off his boot without anyone noticing? What if the servants saw? For his stocking foot had edged beneath her gown and was busy kneading her calf.

"I suspect she needed this reprieve before finding herself saddled with me for the rest of her life."

Eloise leaned forward, clearly fascinated. "Why on earth

would you entertain such a notion? Surely any intelligent young woman would leap at the opportunity to become affianced to a young man such as yourself."

"Ours was a union arranged by our parents when we were but infants," Bridge said. "My lady longs for the excitement of an actress's life, so I encouraged her to go sow those oats. To return to me only when she is convinced it is her destiny."

"You are a most unusual young man," Eloise said.

That is beyond certain, Fallon thought.

"Wouldn't you say, my dear?" Eloise directed her words most pointedly to Fallon, then paused for a closer look. Fallon cursed the candles' illumination. "You are flushed, my dear. I hope you are not falling ill."

"I found the soup a trifle warm," Fallon said breathlessly. Moist prickles of awareness chased up and down her legs, and tiny droplets of perspiration nested between her breasts. She caught a shallow breath, aware of the way breathing caused her breasts to press more fully against the bodice of her gown, the sensitive nipples boldly ripening, begging for Bridge's touch, responding to his lingering gaze by budding into almost unbearable tight knots of tension.

"If you're quite certain you're all right?" Eloise turned her attention back to Bridge, chattering like a peahen as she ate her meal.

Bridge listened and responded only when required as he partook of his meal with gusto. Mrs. Buttle had elected to serve what she considered a "man's meal." Slabs of roast beef drowned in rich dark gravy, with light-as-air Yorkshire pudding and a mountain of fluffy mashed potatoes.

Bridge more than made up for Fallon's lack of appetite. It appeared that his appetite in all things was insatiable, even if his table manners—at least those below the table—left something to be desired.

His gaze moved from Eloise to her, capturing hers with telling intensity as he suggestively licked his lips and lovingly sipped his wine, his wordless actions telling her how he would enjoy the wicked act of licking and sipping her.

Below the table, his foot was now settled firmly in her lap. Fallon knew she could pull her chair back and sever all contact, which is exactly what she ought to do. Instead, she found herself caught up in enjoying the gently undulating waves of pleasure at the increased pressure of his foot against her mound.

She half closed her eyes as she recalled the talented rasp of his tongue against her feminine core, opening her slick inner lips, lapping the honeyed nectar that flowed from within her. His toes were nearly as talented as his fingers, probing, prying, finding their prey, her achy, needy clitoris. As he honed in on that most needful spot she shifted slightly and rocked against him, unable to deny herself the resultant ripples of delight.

Across from her he watched closely, intent on encouraging her pleasure, reading the shallow rise and fall of her breath, increasing the pressure accordingly, until the dam burst and she shuddered and let out a tiny shocked gasp.

Eloise glanced up from her trifle. "Oh, dear. Did something go down the wrong way?"

Fallon swallowed with great effort, then forced a discreet

cough into her napkin. "I believe it must have. I'm all right now."

Eloise subjected her to a searching glance. "You look far more relaxed than earlier. There's nothing like a nice meal at a beautifully appointed table, shared with kindred spirits." Her benevolent smile embraced both Fallon and Bridge before she returned to her dessert.

Chapter Seven

$\mathcal{A}s$ *they retired* to the drawing room at the meal's end, Fallon sent a pointed glance Bridge's way. It was time for him to take his leave. When he ignored her look, she took matters into her own hands.

"I'll see you to your room, Eloise. Bridge, we have an early day tomorrow."

Bridge pulled a little-boy face. "No nightcap to aid our digestion? Surely you don't expect anyone to sleep on such a full stomach."

"I would adore a drop of sherry," Eloise chirped.

"Port for me, please," Bridge said, settling himself on the

settee and stretching his long legs before him toward the fire. Just the memory of that foot against her mons caused the heat to flare in Fallon's cheeks, and she distracted herself by ringing for Franklin to serve their drinks.

"Sherry for Mrs. Gilchrist and port for Mr. Bridgeman, please."

"And f-for yourself, madam?"

"Nothing for me, thank you, Franklin."

"Very g-g-good, madam." The houseman served the drinks, bowed, and left.

Fallon couldn't tear her gaze from the way Bridge held the port glass balanced aloft between his long, talented fingers, admiring the liquor's rich, tawny color in the firelight. The thought of those hands against her skin brought a most wanton image to mind. Tanned, masculine hands, caressing, probing, inflaming her soft white skin, setting her nerve endings on fire, then quenching those flames with his . . .

"Cheers," Bridge said, raising his glass toward her and Eloise. Fallon flushed guiltily, afraid he could read her thoughts. She shifted her gaze to Eloise. Her mother-in-law had seated herself flirtatiously near Bridge on the settee, while Fallon had selected a chair a safe distance from her guest. He *appeared* to be on his best behavior, which for Bridge was often tandem with incorrigible.

"To a most delightful evening, in the company of two of Boston's finest."

Eloise simpered like a young girl. "You are a most charming rake, Mr. Bridgeman. Dare one suppose you might be sowing oats as wildly as your fiancée?"

"Madam, a gentleman never tells."

In between recounting outrageous stories of his youthful exploits, Bridge kept himself busy refilling Eloise's sherry glass until her flaxen head bobbed most unseemly against her chest and her speech was so slurred as to be indecipherable.

"I do believe you've gotten my mother-in-law drunk, Mr. Bridgeman," Fallon said in soft tones.

"So it would appear," Bridge said cheerfully. "Which means she will recall little, if any, of this entire evening's conversation."

"Was that your intent all along?"

"Not at all. Shall I carry her upstairs?"

Fallon blew out a vexed breath. "She hardly seems capable of navigating the journey on her own."

Bridge hefted Eloise in his arms and followed Fallon up to the guest room, where he laid his charge carefully upon the bed.

"I'll say good night to you," Fallon said firmly.

"As you wish," Bridge said. "Good evening. And thank you for the most enjoyable time."

Fallon flushed, knowing he spoke of stimulating her into orgasm directly beneath the unknowing eye of her houseguest.

"You are incorrigible."

"Thank you, my dear. I do my best."

Alone with Eloise, Fallon was relieved that her guest was not a large woman. In a relatively short time she had wrestled her mother-in-law into night attire, then tucked her beneath the covers. The old lady was snoring long before Fallon extinguished the light.

From all sides the house remained quiet, the servants having taken their leave for the evening. It had been a most enjoyable night, Fallon thought as she made her way along the hallway to her room. Perhaps she *had* been reclusive too long. Perhaps it was time she returned to society, began to accept a few invitations.

Her room had been readied by her efficient staff, the fire glowing in the grate, the lamp lit on her dressing table. She splashed a handful of cool water onto cheeks, which still felt unnaturally warm to the touch. Warmth infused by Bridge's look. Bridge's touch.

She released her hair from its usual knot and ran her fingers through the strands, enjoying the light rake of her nails against her scalp, the heavy, sensual swish of her fair, straight hair against the nape of her neck. She unbuttoned her gown, stepped free, and tossed it carelessly across a nearby chair. She stood before the cheval looking glass in her underthings and looked, really looked at her reflection, feeling as if she were seeing herself for the first time. Observing a stranger.

In a sudden bold move she peeled away all of her underpinnings, added them to the chair, and surveyed herself critically. A few faint marks showed on her belly from the life she had so briefly carried and then lost. She felt sadness, acknowledged the loss, whispered her fingertips lightly across her belly, and continued her scrutiny. Full breasts, which had grown hard with milk for the infant, then eventually softened up again with no babe to suckle them.

Yet, how Bridge had enjoyed the suckling. She cupped her

breasts in her hands, recalled their intimacy, his urging her to touch herself. She ran an experimental thumb across the full, soft buds and felt their instant response. A surge of pleasure. A pickle of heat. A vague sense of longing.

She smoothed one hand down the faint curve of her abdomen, and lower into the tangle of curls to that secret place. She felt the warmth. The moisture. The fresh pangs of want. She was fueled with curiosity. How little she knew of her own woman's body.

With a boldness she wouldn't have dreamed herself capable, she repositioned the lantern, seated herself on the edge of the bed facing the looking glass, and spread her legs. Using both hands, she gently probed the pink softness, folded back the outer lips. How lush and pink and ripe she appeared, like the inside of a seashell. Soft pale pink near the entrance, deeper tones farther inside.

The coolness of the room fanned her internal flames as she opened herself wider. Wide enough to see the one place that gave her such intense pleasure. She slid a finger inside her recesses, but found her digit to be too small and short to elicit much delight. However, rubbing the softness of her inner lips with one hand while caressing her nipples with the other brought about the most delightful ripples of slow-building pleasure. Different from the feelings wrought by Bridge's touch. Softer, less intense, yet still very pleasant.

She increased the pressure of her stroke slightly, imagining Bridge in the room, watching her, and felt a fresh outpouring of heated juices from her pussy. Yes, Bridge would enjoy the sensual act of watching her pleasure herself. She imagined his cock swelling against the confines of his trousers as he watched, his eyes dark with passion as he became further aroused.

She rubbed herself faster, increasing the pressure against her clitoris. Oh, that felt far too good. Her movements slowed to a subtle tease. She didn't want to come yet. Not yet! She wanted to continue her thoughts of Bridge. Seeing him watching her. Imagining him unfastening his trousers. Unable to stop himself from seeking his satisfaction as he watched her bring herself to orgasm. She could almost see the swollen redness of his cock, a tiny tear weeping from its eye, the way his hand pumped the organ. His concentrated breathing.

She flicked her clitoris with her middle finger. It was hard and hot and engorged. So responsive; aching for release. She was panting as if she had run a race. Her vagina was streaming, her clitoris pulsing, and with one final rub her body convulsed and she gasped aloud, falling backward on the bed. Deep inside she felt the tremors pulse, slow, and finally subside.

She listened to the shallow rise and fall of her breath as it slowed to normal. She watched the play of shadows on the ceiling. Suddenly, one shadow detached itself from the others. She gasped. And felt the mattress give beneath his weight as Bridge hovered over her.

"No!" Mortification ripped through her. What she had done was private, yet he had been there all along, watching her. She whipped her head from side to side, avoiding his lips.

But his lips trapped hers, his mouth hot and hungry and needy as he took possession. "I love it when a woman isn't afraid to address her own needs." With those words, all of Fallon's shame and embarrassment melted in the heat of Bridge's embrace.

She could feel his hard, aroused cock pulsing against her through his trousers, and suddenly she longed to have him inside her. Her body responded with a fresh outpouring of love juice. She was hot for Bridge, wet for Bridge, and nothing else mattered save that he was there.

"You knew I was watching."

"I . . . No. Though I did imagine how it would feel if you were."

"And how did it feel?"

"It added to the excitement," she admitted, hardly able to credit her honesty. But Bridge did that to her. He stripped away the veneer of polite society, of moral expectations, peeled back everything until she was exposed and vulnerable, with no place to hide, no refuge from simple truth. From shocking, raw honesty.

"I became unbearably aroused watching you," Bridge whispered as he nuzzled her neck, tongued that sensitive cord near her shoulder, plundered the soft indentation of her eve's trough at the base of her throat.

"So I take it." She reached for his cock, touching his hard pulsing length through his trousers. He felt immense. "But you didn't come."

"I thought I'd save it for you. It required immense self-control on my part."

"Such self-control ought not to go unrewarded," Fallon said.

"I couldn't agree more."

He lowered his lips to hers and Fallon gave herself over to the simple pleasure of kissing. She adored the way his lips molded hers, at once firm and soft, coaxing and demanding. The hot, slippery warmth of his tongue invaded her mouth as if he had exclusive rights to every one of her hot, wet, and oh-so-willing orifices.

He slid two fingers inside her, the motion mimicking that of his tongue ravaging the softness of her mouth, and she whimpered and raised her hips invitingly, wanting, needing more. Needing him.

"You are an impatient little thing, aren't you?" Bridge said. "You've already come, yet you can't wait for the next round. Can you bear to wait?" He reached down for a bottle of port.

"I can when I know the wait will be well worth it." She had no idea what he intended. "Haven't you drunk enough?"

"I believe in saving the best for last." As he spoke, he drizzled a thin amber stream of the liquor onto her breasts and belly."

"Bridge, what . . ."

"Shhh," he murmured as he carefully commenced to lap up the golden liquid, his raspy tongue greedy against her breasts. Then her belly. He sipped from her navel as if it were a tiny chalice and he didn't want to waste a drop. "I've been longing to do this all night. Ever since my first sip of port I imagined it thus, warmed by your skin, my two favorite flavors combined into one heady nectar." He trickled more port onto her hips, her mons, rubbed it into her lips, then gorged himself upon her.

Fallon was unable to do a thing except lie there and ride out the storm of passion he unleashed inside her. Orgasm heaped atop orgasm into one mindless, senseless stream of pleasure, the likes of which she'd never imagined. Eventually he stood and urged her to turn over, prone atop the bed.

"What . . . ?" She tried to twist around to face him, but he gentled her, pushed her hair aside, and kissed her nape. Fallon lay still and absorbed the sensations. The prickly coverlet beneath her swollen, sensitive breasts and mons. The cool sticky moisture of port, followed by his adoring tongue's questing heat as it snaked a slow, torturous path down her spine, his hands lightly grazing the globes of her derriere. Followed by his tongue. Licking, lapping, sucking, stirring her to new heights of frenzied anticipation.

With one finger he gently teased the crease, eliciting a sensation almost like tickling, but far more sensual than that. His touch grew bolder, circled the tiny mouth of her anus.

Fallon felt new, more intense sensations as he continued to kiss her back and fondle her rear. She squirmed helplessly, felt her hips rise to his teasing touch, felt herself open in every conceivable part of her being. She was so hot, so wet, so on the edge of something new and different, almost frightening in its intensity.

Bridge shoved his fingers inside her to dampen them, then slid the tip of his pinkie into the opening of her anus. She gasped in shock, felt the slight stretching to accommodate him, then moaned aloud as he withdrew and reinserted that single digit in slow, deliberate penetration.

Desperately she moved with him, rubbed her breasts and her streaming mons against the slightly abrasive coverlet, but her movement only intensified the impact of his motions and increased her frustration.

Bridge leaned over her, still fully dressed, and spoke directly in her ear. "You like that?"

"No. Yes. I don't know. It's different. Strange."

"You're so tight. So beautiful. So virginal. I want to fuck you there."

She froze. "I can't. You're too big. It'll hurt."

"I'd never hurt you."

She heard him tear off his clothing. Then felt his immense, throbbing cock against her derriere. Instead of attempting to penetrate her, she felt him tonguing her, kissing her, loving her. While she was still trying to absorb the kaleidoscopic impact of his attentions, he tugged her backward, lifted her hips, and drove himself into her vagina.

She groaned aloud at the fabulous relief of his cock filling her, deeper than ever before in this new position. His balls slapped her clit as he fucked her fast and furiously. She matched her movements to his, tried to tightened her vagina walls around him, to squeeze him in her depths, but she was so wet she couldn't hold him as he pounded in and out of her, with an intensity so amazing that she nearly forgot to breathe. She reached back and fondled his testicles with one hand, her other hand gliding down to rub the wet slickness of her clitoris. As release flooded through her she screamed, muffling the sound against the bedcover, then screamed again as Bridge dipped his pinkie back inside her anus, deepening the rush of her orgasm.

When he finally came, his entire body shuddered and shuddered again. She felt his muscles convulse against her as she sank exhausted and boneless, deeper into the softness of the mattress.

Chapter Eight

Bridge collapsed atop her, clearly as spent as she was. She could feel his body give the occasional shudder, almost like an aftershock. His arms cradled her in a pleasant way, strangely contrasting with the wild panting of his breath. Or was that hers? She held her breath for a minute, then let it out more slowly. Both of them, she decided. Still cradling her close, Bridge rolled off of her and pulled her with him. They lay there nested like two spoons in a drawer.

Bridge's breathing slowed and softened into a regular pattern and she was afraid he might have fallen asleep. That would never do! What if she fell asleep alongside him? What if someone came upon them together?

"Bridge." She gave him a prod with her elbow. "Bridge, are you asleep?"

"Not yet. Why?"

"You have to go. Quietly, so as not to wake Eloise."

She felt the low rumble of his laughter stir her hair. "She'll sleep through anything. That's why I got her well and truly pickled."

Fallon rolled from his embrace and turned to face him, mere inches away. "You didn't . . . do it the way you said you would."

"No."

"What made you change your mind?"

"You're not ready. Besides, you trusted me. That in itself was more than enough."

Fallon fell silent, pondering Bridge's words. Had he indeed earned her trust? What made him so certain?

And did Bridge trust her? Did he even feel a need to?

The very fact that she couldn't bring herself to ask the question was an ominous sign, she thought. Fighting off panic, she rolled as far as she was able to her side of the bed, her back toward Bridge.

Surely he'd get the hint. Surely he'd get up and leave.

"This is not how it's done, you know," he said in normal, conversational tones. "From physical closeness, you're supposed to move into talking and sharing."

"Not if we don't want to," she said stiffly.

"Very well, then. I'll go first."

"Leave, you mean?" she asked hopefully.

"No, share a little bit of me. Something you can capture in your rendering of me."

"I have more than enough already, thank you. Enough for an entire series."

"You're afraid of getting close, aren't you?" he asked.

"No."

"Remember, we pledged honesty between us."

"Damn you," Fallon said. "Yes, we did. But I don't believe *afraid* is the right word. I'm uncomfortable with the direction of this conversation."

"I hear fear," he said, rolling onto his back and pillowing his arms comfortably behind his head.

"How would you recognize fear? I'll wager you've never been afraid."

"That's one wager you're doomed to lose. I smelled, tasted, and lived with fear every day I was in the war."

"Were you afraid of dying?"

"No. I was afraid my mates' deaths were for naught. And I swore that when I came back, if I came back, I'd never take anything seriously again."

"Hence your frivolous approach to life," Fallon said.

"Exactly. Now, your turn. Why are you so fearful of getting close?"

She was silent for a while. "Every time I allow myself to get close to someone, I lose them," she said finally. "I already know you'll be on your way, hence I won't allow myself to get close to you and experience that loss again."

"Makes sense," Bridge said. "Our actions are typically a reaction to something which has gone before."

She felt movement as he rose from the bed.

"And I do understand, Fallon. You're done with me for the present, thus I'm banished to my lonely outbuilding." His words were followed by the rustle of clothing as he dressed.

"We both need our rest," she murmured. "The portrait is nearly complete, and I don't wish to lose momentum at this stage."

"God, no. Don't dare lose momentum." She felt the mattress shift as he leaned over and pressed a kiss on her unresponsive shoulder.

"Good night, my dear. Sleep well."

"And you."

Bridge made his way silently down the back stairs, out the kitchen door, and across the lawn to Fallon's studio, pausing to gaze up at the nearly full moon. He was quite accustomed to women and their ways, but Fallon's behavior tonight was a puzzler of the finest order. Who would guess that his attempts to share would turn her from a firebrand to an ice shard faster than he could say Montague Bridgeman aloud?

She had obviously lost more than one person who was near and dear. Her body bore signs of having given birth, yet no youngster was in evidence. As for him, surely he was a bigger fraud than his hostess, for didn't he use physical intimacy as a means of getting close while still maintaining his distance? Perhaps it was time he and Fallon both took a risk.

He took a deep breath of the rose-scented night air, then smiled to himself. Didn't those rose petals just leave him with quite the idea?

The next morning, Fallon was surprised to find that the

Captain Mum had beaten her to the breakfast table, looking none the worse for her overindulgence the night before.

"I trust Mrs. Buttle has seen to your needs," Fallon said, knowing she sounded as stiff and stilted as she looked.

"Lord, Fallon, that frock is a sight. It ought to be burned."

"What's wrong with it? It's part of my mourning attire."

"The Captain would never sanction you going about in a death shroud, my dear. I was hoping, from what I witnessed last night, that you'd moved forward in your grief."

Fallon couldn't control the flush that rose to her cheeks. What had she witnessed? Surely not Bridge's antics during their meal. Mercy, surely she hadn't been awakened by the sounds of their rutting! Fallon knew she had been exceptionally uncontrolled.

"I'm not sure what you mean."

"You've taken on a commission; instilled some life back into this household and your days. And your subject is a most interesting young man. He allowed himself to be the main prize in an auction I arranged."

Fallon choked on her tea. "Really? What manner of auction?"

"My auxiliary is attempting to purchase new books for the library. We want all young people, most particularly young women, to have access to reading materials. To be kept abreast of changes afoot, like that Victoria Woodruff and her movement for free love."

Fallon eyes widened. "You support Mrs. Woodruff?"

"Most certainly. And I didn't wish to embarrass your guest last night by thanking him for his contribution to our successful venture. He fetched a healthy sum, by the way, from your friend Mrs. Stark. I bid against her for a while, simply to drive the bidding as high as possible. Please keep that to yourself."

"Of course."

"I'm quite certain she'll tell you all about it, once you pry yourself away from this self-imposed exile." He mother-in-law delicately blotted her lips with her napkin and rose. "I must be on my way. You know, I had an ulterior motive for stopping in last night. I had fully intended to insist you join me on the Cape, but I'm relieved to know that my intervention is not required. And that you're making your own amusement."

Fallon rose as well and pressed a kiss to the old woman's cheek. "I've always felt lucky to have you for a mother-in-law. You've been like a mother to me in many ways over the years."

"I know, my dear. And I was glad to do so, since you lost your own mother. Watch yourself with young Bridgeman. He acts the wastrel as if born to the role, but he fought in the war. And though he returned unscarred on the outside, I suspect inside of him is a very different matter."

FALLON SEEMED SUBDUED and pensive when she arrived at the studio, a manservant with a breakfast tray following closely. She was wearing a shapeless black gown that bleached all the color from her face and made her resemble a crow. Bridge wondered if her intent was to render herself as unattractive as possible, thus avoiding any further attempts at intimacy on his part.

If so, it was a foiled attempt. For he knew what luscious

curves and creases and juicy orifices simmered just below the surface of the ugly frock. It would take far more than a stiff, shapeless dress for Fallon to make herself unappealing. As a matter of fact, it had quite the opposite effect: he couldn't wait to divest her of the hideous garment.

Her manservant placed the tray upon the table, lifted the silver dome from an impressive plate of eggs, pancakes, sweetbreads, sausage, and steak, then disappeared, leaving them alone.

"You're not joining me." Bridge felt obliged to state the obvious.

"No, I've eaten already." She reached for her voluminous smock. "I'll just ready my things. We can proceed at your leisure."

"Typically, you're very impatient to begin."

Fallon forced what sounded like a hollow laugh. "It's silly, really. I always feel obliged to start with an abrupt, almost frantic plunge, just to ensure I still have the knack." As she spoke she busied herself mixing daubs of paints on her palette, alternately frowning her displeasure or smiling her delight. The room was so still, the silence between them so intense, that Bridge was certain he could hear the swish of the bristles against the palette, giving rise to another source of inspiration. He took a thoughtful bite of his breakfast.

"From viewing your other works, I'd say you have far more than a knack."

"At any rate, as I approach the beginning of the end, I tend to slow right down, almost reluctant to bring the project to a close. It's difficult to let go, I suppose. To say nothing of having to face the daunting task of starting something new—staring at that pristine white canvas, seeking inspiration."

Bridge wondered if that was the point at which she had found herself when he'd entered the picture. "That must play havoc on your models."

"Up until now my models have all been inanimate, with no voice to complain about the unreasonable hours they must serve."

"Still, you always have time constraints, have you not? The drooping head of a flower suddenly loses all its petals. The perfect piece of fruit begins to decay."

"Are you threatening to go to seed on me?"

"Only if you proceed to be unreasonable." He finished his meal and pushed himself to his feet. "A quick trip to the privy and I'm at your disposal."

Fallon nodded distractedly, her attention riveted on the canvas on her easel. Bridge hoped she didn't find the likeness of more interest than the flesh-and-blood version. As a matter of fact, he'd see to it.

The door closed behind Bridge and Fallon let out a pent-up breath as she stared at her unsteady hands. The portrait was nearing completion. Soon her life would return to normal, normal being dull and quiet and stodgy there in the country. But safe. Hadn't safety always been the thing she held most dear? If it was excitement she craved, she needed only to relocate to her townhouse. But would she find living in the city any more appealing? In truth, a future without Bridge held very little appeal at all, no matter where she called home.

She knew Bridge must be puzzled by her sudden coolness,

but she felt her only option was to remain aloof and unattached, not to let him know just how instrumental he'd been in bringing her back to life. Back to herself. If he was in any way privy to that knowledge, then he would be privy to other things, as well. Like the fact that her trust was the least of her gifts to him. And the fact that her heart, her love, he also possessed. These were things he must never know.

She started at the sound of Bridge pointedly clearing his throat. How had he done that—crept so quietly into the room, disrobed, and posed without her noticing? How had her thoughts carried her so far away?

"Perfect," she said in forced cool tones. "You have a good memory for your pose." What she really meant was that he was perfect. Perfect masculine beauty. Perfect inspiration. Far more than the perfect lover. Her hands flew as if guided by angels. Never had her work seemed so effortless, the results so breathtakingly flawless, as if powers beyond hers guided her every move.

As if the love she felt for Bridge poured from the tip of her brush, spilled out onto the canvas, and took on a life and power all its own. Passion and inspiration rushed through her veins, rendering her capable of much more than she had ever dreamed.

Painting Bridge and loving Bridge. The two acts blurred and became one, with a result she found humbling. She'd been granted two momentous gifts: the ability to paint like never before, and the ability to love like never before.

When she finally laid down her palette and brush, she realized her fingers were cramped, her body totally drained, her limbs so weak that they were no longer able to support her.

Somehow, Bridge knew. For without a word or even an exchange of looks, he was there at her side, catching her as she swayed backward. Lowering her to a chair.

"You're all done," he said.

She nodded, unable to muster the strength to speak.

"May I see?"

She managed to nod one more time, then held her breath as he turned toward the portrait.

He stood rigidly, simply looking.

She held her breath, longing for yet fearing his reaction.

Fallon felt as if the world stood still, the tides, the moon, the stars, the rotation of the planet. That clocks no longer ticked and sand lay still in the hourglass. It was the longest, most drawn out few moments of her existence. It could have been seconds or hours, she had no way to judge.

Finally Bridge turned to her.

She caught her breath.

He knows! How could he possibly not?

She felt as if the love that flowed from her to him, the inspiration she received as a reward for that love, was pathetically obvious. She couldn't meet his gaze! Couldn't face what was bound to be his pity. Instead, she looked away.

Bridge knelt down beside her, grasped her chin between his finger and thumb, and forced her gaze to meet his.

"I am rendered speechless," he said. "It is truly magnificent. I am honored to have been your simple subject."

She found it impossible to speak past the lump of emotion

caught in her throat. At any rate, words seemed totally unnecessary.

"And now," Bridge said, "you must allow me to paint you."

She found her voice then. "Bridge, you don't paint. Do you?"

"Indulge me," he said, the husky timbre of his voice feathering the sensitive nerve endings on the back of her neck and making it impossible for her to refuse him anything. He took her hand, drew her to her feet, and guided her to the velvet-and-satin-draped settee where he had posed tirelessly for so many hours. From behind it, he pulled out a bulky burlap sack. When he upended the sack, the air was awash with the scent of roses. Thousands of rose petals floated through the air and added their texture to the puddle of satin and velvet.

Fallon could only stare transfixed as they landed. Every rainbow hue of red and orange and pink and yellow and mauve and white, some bruised, others flawless. The end result mimicked the soft, still sweetness of a painting by Monet.

She crushed a few petals between her fingers, inhaling their dewy, perfumed fragrance. Intoxicating. Was this real, or was it simply a dream?

It certainly felt real. As real as Bridge's fingers against her nape, unfastening the buttons of her gown, tugging it down her shoulders, her hips, and urging her to step forward, free of its confines. He continued to divest her of her garments, layers of petticoats, stockings, and more intimate apparel, until she found herself lying naked, sunlight spilling through the window and warming her skin. As she luxuriated in the rose petals' softness, their scent surrounded her, enfolded her, intoxicated her.

This must be what heaven is like, Fallon thought, floating on a cloud among the angels, transported to an unnamed state of total bliss.

Was this even real, here in her studio with Bridge? Perhaps she had imagined the entire incident, beginning with Anna's visit. Perhaps she had simply painted the beautiful young man of her heart and wished him come to life. Perhaps . . .

She felt the soft whisper of sable bristles against the sensitive skin on the inside of her arm, before it moved to the even more sensitive skin of her breast. She glanced at Bridge. The brush was dry, no line of paint followed its journey, yet her skin burned as surely as if he touched her with a candle flame.

"Beautiful," he murmured as the brush, positioned between his clever fingers, followed the dips and curves of her upper body. She felt her back arch slightly, encouraging his charting of her feminine shape.

He stared at the brush's pathway with rapt concentration, his eyes following its course, his gaze devouring her. He licked his lips, but she doubted that he was even aware of it. Her own lips quivered in reaction. She longed to lean forward and press her mouth to his, yet didn't dare to move lest she break his concentration.

He picked up a second brush, larger and stiffer and slightly more abrasive against her skin. He outlined each areola, tracing around and around the soft round shape, watching in fascination as her nipples puckered in reaction. She noticed his response, his cock stirring and coming to life, growing hard and stiff even as she stared at it.

The paintbrushes continued their assault against her skin, following the valley between her breasts to the rounded softness of her belly, where he explored the dip of her navel.

She giggled. "That tickles. So does that."

Now he was tracing the crease at the top of her thigh, beginning at her hipbone and inching his way toward her mons. The bristles of the brushes were deeper brown in tone than the fair curls they approached, and rigidly straight in contrast to the springy nest guarding her entranceway.

She felt her legs relax, and part slightly in shy invitation. She grew wet with wanting. His cock looked delicious. How she longed to dip her head forward, to feel its soft velvety tip between her lips. But he moved out of reach, moving down to paint her feet.

Fallon inhaled harshly as he dragged the soft bristles between each toe and circled the bone on the inside of her ankle. Moving to the outer anklebone, he branded her there as well, then tickled her bare sole. Damp prickles of awareness ran up her legs and lodged in that secret cavern that was already damp with desire, hot with need.

Like a maestro playing his favorite instrument, Bridge grew more bold. He bent over her, one paintbrush chasing up her leg, the second one torturing her nipples.

She rolled her head from side to side, no longer able to lie still for his attentions. "Bridge," she entreated. "Enough. I beg you, have pity."

He loomed over her. "Put you out of your misery, you mean?"

"Yes, please."

"Yet you painted me for days. You had me sit here naked hour after hour, your unmoving subject, dying for your slightest touch, which you denied me. And you can't bear to have me paint you for a few short minutes?"

"It feels like a lifetime."

He gestured to the completed portrait on the easel. "One day the whole world will see me as you did. Yet no one shall ever see you through my eyes, right here, right now. Warm, willing, and wanton."

She glanced over his shoulder, past the flesh-and-blood man, to his likeness. "As I am for your eyes alone, so shall be your likeness."

Bridge shook his head as he lowered himself atop her. "One day, my dear, you shall betray me, expose my naked vulnerability to the world. In a way that I can never expose yours."

He punctuated his words with a kiss that swallowed her protest and chased all other thoughts from her mind.

With one sure movement he thrust himself inside her. She raised her hips to receive him, felt herself stretch and welcome his size, aware of the way something hard and primitive guided his movements. As if his possession of her had the power to drive all else out of her mind and out of their lives. As if the simple sex act could hold the rest of the world at bay.

She held on to his hips and rode out the storm with which

he entered and withdrew and reentered her, possessing her as no man ever had, a sad desperation in his actions. Their mutual climax was bittersweet, and afterward they held each other tenderly among the rose petals. As if both hearts knew this was the last time they would lie thus.

Chapter Nine

Fallon didn't know how she could bear to let Bridge go. She felt as if a part of herself was about to be dismembered. In desperation she clung to him, long before he physically loosened her grip and slowly slid to his feet. Free at her side, he stood looking down upon her, his expression unreadable.

She knew the rose petal mattress was bruised beyond salvage as were her heart and her soul. Yet she didn't regret one second of any of it, including the delightfully tender throbbing between her legs, a reminder of the heights of passion to which Bridge lifted her. Or the pain which she knew would follow.

But she realized now that it was fear of loss which had

held her back. It had hampered her creativity, her zest for life. Loss was simply another fact of life. She knew that now. And so she could proceed, knowing that she would miss Bridge terribly, but that she would survive.

"Well?" she asked, meaning, Was this the end? Was he preparing to leave her so soon?

"We have a day together remaining, do we not?"

"We do." She pulled herself to a sitting position, no longer uncomfortable in her state of undress. Bridge had given her that, and, so much more.

"And you're done with me sitting for you, correct?"

Her heart plummeted at his words. Yes, his obligation to her was well and truly fulfilled. "That is correct as well."

"So, since I have been so utterly amenable, I decree it is my turn to choose."

"To choose what?"

"How we should spend our last day together."

"What would you have us do?"

"I would have us journey to Boston."

"Oh, I . . ." Fallon balked. It had been so long since she had traveled to the city.

"Don't turn skittish on me, Fallon. I wish to experience a little culture, and who better to have by my side?"

"What sort of culture?"

"There is an exhibit of paintings and sculpture at the Boston Athenaeum. I wish to view it with you."

"An art exhibit?"

"Precisely. We shall view the exhibit, dine in style, and perhaps take in a play."

Fallon pursed her lips thoughtfully. His request was certainly not outrageous, nor what she might have expected. Still, she sensed something not quite ringing true with his plans. Something she couldn't quite put her finger on, but that set off her internal warning signals.

"Why me? The city is chock-full of eligible young women who would surely swoon at the chance to spend a day by your side."

"I don't happen to enjoy the company of swooners. I do, however, delight in your presence. Look upon it as a challenge: an opportunity to educate a rogue such as myself, to impart a modicum of culture into my heathen life."

"You're not nearly as much of the rogue as you let on."

He placed a cool finger against her lips to silence her. "I pray you, don't divulge my secret. A man has his reputation to uphold, after all." She noticed he didn't refer to himself as a gentleman. Quite right, given that he was anything but. She stirred restlessly, reluctant to go, reluctant to stay.

His next words gave her pause. "Promise you won't run off on me in the night."

"What on earth gives you cause to say such a thing?"

He didn't shift so much as a fraction, yet his closeness intensified. "As you know me, so do I know you. And how you choose to deal with things which make you uncomfortable."

Fallon was taken aback by his astuteness. Was she so transparent? "By running?"

Bridge nodded sagely. "Flight is one way out."

"Are there others?"

"Of course. I fled into the reality of war. Put paid to 'fight or flight,' for I did both."

"Do you wish to talk about your days as a soldier?"

"No. Do you wish to talk about why you choose to run?"

"I don't choose to run. I choose to feel safe."

Bridge nodded. "Everyone deserves the chance to feel safe. Is that why you still wear your dead husband's ring?"

Nervously, Fallon twisted it on her finger. "It feels respectful to his memory."

"Yet you are no longer married."

"It is customary."

"I think you ought to take it off. To move forward."

"Never!"

"Your choice." He reached out and tugged her to her feet. "Come and dress, and we'll make arrangements; inform the servants we leave at first light."

"I'm quite capable of doing so on my own. I've been doing so for quite some time, you know."

"Still, I do believe I'll accompany you, if you have no objections."

"Why on earth might I object?"

After her conversation with the groom, requesting the carriage be made ready for their journey, Bridge followed her to her room and rifled her closet, choosing what he wished her to wear the following day. Then she did object.

"I can't possibly wear that out in public before dark." Fallon stared in horror at the deep ruby gown, with a sheen that alternately darkened or shimmered, depending upon the light. She knew all too well how it fit, snugging her bosom and her hips, emphasizing her curves and her femininity. She'd bought it on a lark a long time ago but had never worn it. Now that she was a widow she had never expected even to consider donning it, yet for Bridge . . .

He made her feel that she *could* wear the dress. That her mourning days were behind her; that she was still attractive enough to be so arrayed.

He leaned indolently against her wall, one booted foot crossed over the other, his arms folded with masculine precision against his chest, his pose so typically, universally male, it was all she could do not to laugh aloud. "Did you not dictate what *I* wore for our sessions together?"

Fallon felt a slow flush of color from her neck to her face as she recalled the bold way she had initially told him to strip. Who was that woman masquerading in her body? Should she go? Should she stay?

"So you see," he continued, "it is my turn to choose your wardrobe for tomorrow's outing. 'Tis only fair."

"I'm not sure that fairness is part of the bargain," Fallon said primly. "I've agreed to the excursion. To what else must I agree?"

"To getting a good night's sleep, so you're well rested," Bridge said in husky tones. He leaned forward, and she was sure he was about to kiss her good night. But at the last minute he wheeled about, leaving Fallon deeply disappointed.

Their last night together. She'd thought for certain he'd devise some way that necessitated they spend the night together, and she wondered how it would feel to fall asleep in each other's arms. To waken in the night with the warmth of his body stretched alongside her, his hand resting in the indentation of her waist or possessively cupping her breast while she slept. She'd never know if he slept restlessly, kicked the bedcovers loose, or talked in his sleep. So strong was her longing that she actually opened her mouth to summon him back. Fortunately, sanity saved her from making a total idiot of herself.

Early the following morning, after much debate with herself, Fallon donned the gown of Bridge's choosing. She had to admit that the ruby hue did bring forth spectacular color in her skin and her hair. The sensual swish of the fabric made her feel alluring as she moved back and forth before the mirror. Surely she had been shrouding herself too long in black. She'd forgotten the depth of green in her eyes, the pink of her cheeks and lips, the glint of red gold in her hair when touched by the sun. And to think she called herself an artist. 'Twas almost shameful.

Mrs. Buttle, ever one to fuss, had packed a huge basket of treats for the trip. Though it would take but a few hours to reach the city, that good woman had packed enough to last them a fortnight should they become marooned along the way.

Fallon had nervously fussed too long with her hair and her jewelry, and as a result was ten minutes past their agreed meeting time. She found the carriage in readiness, a restless Bridge pacing alongside it in the drive.

"At last. I was just about to come fetch you."

She paused, taken aback at the agitation upon his handsome face. "You really weren't sure about my presence, despite my agreeing to accompany you, were you?"

As if aware that he revealed far too much, Bridge flashed her a lascivious look. "I must say, you were worth waiting for. You look stunning."

"Thank you." His words brought to mind how very long it had been since she had cared how she looked, as seen through the eyes of a man. "I wasn't aware we were on that strict a schedule."

"One wouldn't necessarily expect it of a rogue such as myself, but punctuality is one of the few virtues to which I can lay claim."

"I'll remember that," Fallon said lightly, then regretted her words. She made it sound as if they would have other assignations in the future, when they both knew this was to be their last time together.

Franklin handed her inside the carriage, and cast a dark look in Bridge's direction as he tucked a traveling robe about her. Fallon bit back her laughter. As if such a flimsy covering might afford protection from Bridge, should he choose to ravage her. The weighty basket of foodstuffs was placed alongside her pointedly, a physical barrier between herself and her guest.

"Thank you, Franklin," she said dryly, aware that the man was only protecting what he saw as her virtue and reputation. If only he knew 'twas far too late to reclaim either.

"Y-you're quite certain that will b-b-be all, madam?"

"I'm far too long in the tooth to require a chaperon, thank you, Franklin. At any rate, we'll be back in time for a late evening meal. Please make certain Mrs. Buttle knows that, for I fear she packed enough food for a far longer journey."

"Very g-good, madam. Godspeed." With utmost reluctance, he stepped aside and gave Bridge room to swing up inside.

"Quaint," Bridge said as he shut the door, and the coachman started the carriage forward.

"No manservant lobbying for your virtue at your place of residence?" Fallon asked.

"Hardly. By now they're quite accustomed to my scandalous actions."

"What scandalous actions might those be?" In truth she could hardly imagine anything more scandalous than the past six days. But she had a feeling Bridge's behavior had been circumspect in comparison to his norm.

"Actions too shocking for a lady such as yourself to even know about."

"Indeed." Fallon leaned back against the seat and slanted a sideways glance at Bridge. Perhaps he made love to two women at the same time? Or a man and a woman together? No, Bridge was far too demanding to wait his turn with a lover. Perhaps he and his partners role-played? Or took turns securing each other with silken bonds?

She had to admit, the thought of tying Bridge up, rendering him helpless for her attentions, held a certain amount of appeal. Besides, it was the only time he would ever be anything close to helpless.

If she could tie him up, what would she like to do to him first? She closed her eyes and allowed her imagination free rein. Tickle him with a feather, perhaps, the way he had tickled her with the sable brushes. She crossed and uncrossed her legs, aware of her body's instant response to any suggestion of her and Bridge together, clothed or unclothed.

"Catch!" He flipped a shiny penny her way.

Fallon reached out and caught it midair. "What's this for?"

"Your thoughts, of course. They look much too delicious not to share."

She felt a warm flush deepen the color of her cheeks. Was she so transparent? "You don't know that for a certainty."

"But I'm prepared to pay for the information."

She lobbed the penny back. "I'm afraid you can't afford me. My thoughts are worth far more than a penny."

"Tell me anyway. It's our last day together. What would you do to me? Or have me do to you?"

"Do you ever think of anything besides sex?"

"Certainly. But rarely when I'm in your presence."

Her blush deepened. "Really, Bridge . . ."

"Really, Fallon," he replied, as if her words had been a question. One that demanded an affirmative response.

"I was simply anticipating our outing," Fallon replied primly.

'Twas true enough. Now that they were under way, she felt anticipation for the adventure ahead quiver through her. Time enough, once Bridge was gone, to mourn the loss. For now, life beckoned, a day filled with sunshine and promise. A day with a most handsome and personable companion. Impossible that she could ever have foreseen such a happenstance. She smiled a secret smile, thinking she had much for which to thank Anna.

Bridge observed Fallon from beneath lowered lids. Besides a flush of anticipation, a small, almost secretive smile hovered upon her luscious lips. He resisted the urge to scoot over that wretched basket between them and kiss it away.

"What, if I may be so bold as to ask, do you find so amusing?"

"If you may be bold? What could possibly hold you back?"

"Your good influence."

"Hah!" Catching him by surprise, she whisked the picnic basket out of the way, wriggled along the seat till her thigh brushed his, and laid her head upon his shoulder.

"I confess to a feeling of overwhelming happiness. And eternal gratitude to Anna for her birthday gift."

"'Tis a rare good friend who knows so well just what one needs." His arm cradled her against him.

"I think you must also be a rare good friend, then. For you always seem to know what I need at any given time. Often ahead of myself."

As she spoke, she boldly inched her skirt up till its hem was above her knees. He could see the white band of skin between the tops of her stockings and the jewel tone of her gown. He watched her lick her lips in a most suggestive way, her gaze never leaving his. "I must confess to a most serious oversight on my part. I seem to have accidentally left off my knickers."

"Mrs. Gilchrist! Are you attempting to seduce me?"

"If you have to ask, I'm not doing it right, am I? It just seemed that on our last day together, with a long, boring carriage ride, we ought to do something to while away the time." She pushed her skirt back down. "My apology."

"There is nothing to forgive. Don't you know most men dream of a moment like this? Finding themselves seduced, rather than the seducer?"

"Really?" She widened her eyes and inched her skirt back up above her knees. "So I'm not making a total hash of things?"

"Quite the contrary. I find it impossible to concentrate on anything other than your pantiless state."

As he spoke, Bridge jockeyed himself into position before her and pushed her knees apart. He could see nought but the shadowy triangle beyond the milk-white satin of her thighs. Her woman smell was rich and musky and elemental, like freshly turned soil after a rainfall. A scent so primal it touched his very core.

He kissed her lips, a deep, bruising kiss of possession, as if ensuring any who kissed her after him would pale by comparison. As if his possession was the only one she would ever need or desire. She tasted so sweet, even as she kissed him back with a passion and heat that belied her sweetness. He heard the deep murmur of desire in the back of her throat and it sent the blood surging through his veins.

The skin of her inner thighs was incredibly soft to his touch. Hard to fathom that such softness really existed. Her heat beckoned, teased, promised delights not of this earth.

He pushed her skirt up higher as his mouth followed the

pathway traced by his fingertips. Licking, nibbling, gorging himself on her heat and her scent until he reached that most delicious of all wellsprings, her feminine core.

As he feasted, he murmured, "So hot. So wet. So delicious." His tongue darted out, flicking the quivering lips of her labia, teasing her clitoris. She writhed in response, her fingers tangled in his hair, her hips gyrating in time to the rhythm of his lips and his tongue. Pushing against him. Pulling away. Pushing back. He grasped her hips and held her still, felt the rush of love juices filling his mouth, the engorging heat rushing to the surface of her mons. The sweet, satisfying taste of her. He felt her quivering inner response, the minor eruptions that signaled the beginning of her orgasm. He played to the rhythm, slowing the tempo, then increasing it tenfold.

She went crazy beneath him, bucking and panting, and when she came, it seemed more intense than ever before. Perhaps they had each other's rhythms perfectly in sync, for he nearly lost it as well at the cry of her release, the saturation of her juices, the throb of her mons, pulsing against his wet and swollen lips. He backed away and let her catch her breath as the tremors subsided, licking his lips, enjoying the fragrance and the flavors of her.

Almost reluctantly he smoothed her skirt back down over her knees. "And that, my dear, is only one of the things that can happen when a lady leaves the house without her knickers."

She rubbed his hard, throbbing length, which strained the front of his trousers. In mock innocence, she batted her eyes. "Such a shame you're wearing yours."

"Indeed," Bridge said dryly. "Not to worry, I'm sure it's a situation we shall be able to remedy before the day is out."

Fallon wriggled back against her seat with a satisfied smile. "I shall look forward to the event with much anticipation."

Bridge laughed and kissed her soundly. "A fact of which I have little doubt."

Chapter Ten

They reached Boston just as that fine city appeared to be shaking itself awake. Sequestered in the country, Fallon had forgotten what a hive of activity the city could be. The air crackled with bustling energy, positively infectious, urging them to hurry. Hurry and what? Fallon didn't care to rush; not when the day's end signaled the final curtain of her time with Bridge.

The air was rife with the tang of coal smoke from the many chimneys, combined with the smells of fish and sharp cheeses from the market at Faneuil Hall. Fallon leaned forward in her seat and peered out the carriage window, feeling an excitement she hadn't felt for years. As the wife of Captain Gilchrist she'd been expected to act in a certain way, to meet the expectations of Boston's upper-crust, Beacon Hill set. After his death, she'd existed in some sort of torpor. Yet here she was now, fully awake, fully alive, and eager to eat her fill from the bowl of life.

"Can we stop at the park?" she asked Bridge. "I always loved the park, especially in the springtime."

He appeared mildly amused by her enthusiasm. "We can do whatever you wish, my dear."

She beamed at him. "That's ever so kind. Particularly as this day was yours. I shan't take over. Really, I shan't." She sat back, hands folded primly in her lap, eyes downcast.

Bridge laughed aloud. "I don't know whatever gave you the idea that meek and complacent fits you, Fallon. It's totally at odds with the woman I have discovered."

"The woman you brought back to life, you mean."

"You weren't dead, my dear. Merely sleeping. And all it took was . . ." He leaned forward with deliberate intent, and Fallon felt a flutter of excitement in her breasts.

"A kiss from the Prince?"

He brushed his lips across hers in a light, reverent fashion. "I'm hardly a prince. And if it hadn't been me, it would have been some other lucky chap. You're far too vibrant and alive to sleepwalk through life."

"I was not sleepwalking," Fallon said, uncomfortable at how closely his thoughts paralleled her own.

"You were a mere shadow of the woman I see before me today."

"Is there something wrong with shadows?"

"It depends on whether you're using them to hide."

Bridge stuck his head out the carriage window and called an order to the driver.

"What was that about?"

"Following milady's request. To the park first."

"Bridge, you don't have to do everything to please me, you know."

"Why not, when pleasing you has the added benefit of also pleasing myself."

The carriage halted near the lagoon. Bridge alighted and turned to assist Fallon down.

She took a deep, appreciative sniff as she glanced around at their surroundings. "It's beautiful here. I had forgotten how truly picturesque."

"You're not afraid of water, I hope."

"Certainly not. Why do you ask?"

"I thought it would be fun to rent a rowboat and take it out on the lagoon."

Fallon clapped her hands in delight. "Bridge, what a lovely idea. The Captain . . ." Her words trailed away.

"The Captain," Bridge prompted.

"He spent most of his time away at sea. Rowing about the lagoon was hardly his idea of a delightful recreational pursuit."

"But it is yours?"

"The wife bows to her husband's decree."

Bridge shook his head. "Somehow, I can't envision you bowing to anyone's decree, my dear."

"You'd be surprised," Fallon murmured.

But Bridge was no longer within earshot. He was locked in negotiations with the man at the concession stand. Money exchanged hands, and before she knew it, she was handed into the rowboat and settled on the wooden seat. Bridge took a seat across from her and picked up the oars. The fellow pushed them off. Almost immediately they began rowing about in circles.

"Bridge, what on earth are you about? Or do you even know?"

"Shush," he said. "I'm attempting to impress you with my seamanship skills."

"How about showing off how you navigate in a straight line, before I grow dizzy?"

"I like you dizzy and off balance," he said with a lecherous grin.

"You wouldn't necessarily appreciate fishing me out should I flounder overboard."

"On the other hand, I'm quite partial to you wearing water-soaked garments which cling to you like a second skin."

Fallon tipped the brim of her bonnet and gazed skyward. "No hint of rain, I fear. You'll have to be content with me as I am."

"No quarrels in that quarter, either. You look extremely fetching, I must say."

"Mmmmmmm." Fallon leaned back and trailed her fingers through the sun-warmed water of the lagoon. "I feel incredibly relaxed."

"I should hope so," Bridge said, his eyes moving across her

in a most leisurely fashion. Fallon felt herself responding to the message in his gaze as his eyes moved over her breasts, as lovingly as if she were privy to his touch. How did he manage that? Make her achingly aware of him, of the pleasures his body could bring hers, even though a foot or more separated them.

"You're rowing much better," she said, slyly sliding her foot from her slipper beneath the hem of her frock. "Were you on your school's rowing team?"

"Hardly," Bridge said with a laugh. "I was far too busy drinking my way through my lessons."

"I see." Fallon edged her foot across the distance between them, and onto his seat. He sat with his legs apart, concentrating on his rowing skills. The snug lines of his trousers cradled his manhood and emphasized his masculinity. Fallon inched her foot toward him, recalling that night at her home when Captain Mum had dined with them. Clearly it was time to return the attention.

"Have you ever rowed?" he asked pleasantly.

"Me? No. Why?"

"Come sit here, I'll teach you how."

Her intended target was instantly abandoned in the face of this new offer.

"Really?"

"Certainly." He spread his legs wider. "Give me your hand."

Fallon did as she was bade, placing her hand in his.

"Now, half stand and swing about." He guided her actions, holding her fast, till she landed with a quiet squeak in front of him, nested between those long, strong legs.

"I like this," Bridge said, his words hot on the exposed nape of her neck.

Fallon leaned back against him, conscious of his strength, his body's warmth, stoked by the midmorning sunshine. Contentment washed through her.

"I like it, as well."

He continued to row and her body followed the motions of his, forward and back, as he pulled at the oars.

"Good," he said. "Now take the oars from me. Excellent."

She grasped the wooden oars, finding their weight and balance unwieldy. They started to spin from her grip until Bridge's hands closed over hers, steadying the motion.

She could feel every inch of him pressed against every inch of her. From the way his legs snugged against hers to the juncture of his thighs nestled against her bottom, to how his strong chest and shoulders and arms cradled her. She felt small and delicate and protected. Safe. Infinitely safe.

"All right?" he said, his husky tones in her ear causing a shuddering ripple to chase through her.

"Very all right." Fallon half turned, and was rewarded when he buried his lips against her cheek, her neck, the pressure intensifying the waves of longing that ran through her.

"Is this how one rows?" she asked, as she released one oar and cupped his cheek, guiding his lips to the supersensitive dip between her shoulder and neck.

She could feel the stirring of his cock lodged against her bottom and couldn't resist reaching behind herself, fondling his length with her free hand. She exhaled as he let out a breathy moan.

"Someone has to steer the boat, my love."

"I'm not sure I'm capable."

"Nor I." He released the oar she still held, and wrapped his free hand around her midsection.

"So if you have one oar and I have the other . . ."

"Teamwork of the finest order," he said. "Unbeatable."

"We are the only ones out here," she murmured.

"It's early," Bridge said.

"How stable do you think the boat is?"

"Not stable enough for what you're thinking, you wanton woman, you."

"What a shame," Fallon murmured, still cradling his hard cock. "I hate to think of this going to waste."

"Fear not. Like the phoenix from the ashes, it, too, will rise again."

"I suppose you ought to teach me how to row," Fallon murmured.

"First, I suggest you let go of my balls and take hold of both oars."

"Spoilsport."

"Witch."

Abruptly Bridge released her and pulled both oars safely into the boat with them. Then he picked her up and spun her about so she faced him, straddling his knees.

"Bridge, you're going to cause us to tip."

"I thought you trusted me."

"*You* thought," Fallon said. "I never said so, did I?"

He kissed her long and hard. Fallon had just melted into him when she heard the sound of childish giggles nearby. A second rowboat drifted into sight with a family of four. The two young children were obviously amused by the sight of Fallon on Bridge's lap, although the father winked and raised his oar in greeting.

"Oh, dear," Fallon murmured, leaning against his chest.

"No privacy," Bridge said. "At least not the sort we have grown used to this past week."

A week in which everything had proved possible, and nothing was taboo.

Fallon fell quiet.

"What's the matter, love?" Bridge asked.

"Nothing . . . Just . . . Where did the time go?"

He pulled out his pocket watch and glanced at it. "It's still early. We'll have all the time your heart desires to spend at the gallery."

"That's good." But not all the time her heart desired to spend with Bridge. Taking care not to upset the boat, she shifted off Bridge's knee and back to her own seat. She leaned back, stared up at the sky, and trailed her fingers through the water pensively. Bridge, ever sensitive to her moods, let her be, whistling tunelessly as he rowed them about the lagoon.

There was no point in being sad, she decided, or even pensive. She pulled her fingers from the water and flicked the droplets at Bridge. At first he didn't seem to notice, so she repeated the move.

"Hey!" This time she got his attention. "What are you doing?"

"Cooling you off," she said flirtatiously. "You look hot."

"I'll show you cooling off." Deftly he angled the paddle

through the water. A thin stream hit its mark. Droplets rained upon her. She laughed and splashed him back.

"Truce?" he mockingly manipulated the oar her way. She sat forward, grabbed the oar, and tried to wrestle it from him, to no avail. She succeeded only in holding fast to one end while he maneuvered the other, using it to draw her forward. She let go, throwing her hands up in mock surrender. "You have an unfair advantage."

"And I'll use it every time, so be careful what you start."

Or, what I end, Fallon thought.

Their driver delivered them to the Boston Athenaeum, which was nearly deserted inside. Their footsteps rang hollowly throughout each chamber as they made their way through the exhibit.

Bridge paused before a painting of a dark-haired woman in a red velvet dress sipping a cup of tea. Fallon thought it ironic that the piece was titled *Destiny.* Was Bridge her destiny?

"Perhaps someday I shall see a show of Fallon Gilchrist works here," he said, his head cocked thoughtfully.

"That's very kind of you, but I've hardly reached a level to rival John William Waterhouse."

"I disagree. Besides, I have it on good authority that there is a movement afoot to educate and support the achievements of women artists in Boston."

"Really? Then times truly have changed since I took up painting."

"William Rimmer and William Morris Hunt are even offering classes for women."

"Should I enroll?" Fallon asked lightly.

"My dear, you have no further need of tutelage. You are simply ahead of your time."

"Just because you like my work . . ."

"My mother is on the committee here. Just say the word and I'll tell her about you."

Fallon gripped his arm harder than necessary. "Absolutely not!" Her grip gentled, but not her expression. "You misled me, Mr. Bridgeman."

Bridge gave her a puzzled glance. "How so?"

"You pretended to be in total ignorance, requiring my presence to educate you in the cultural realm. Now you tell me your mother is on the committee here. Hence, you are hardly a cultural heathen."

Bridge drew her arm through his. "You caught me out. I truly just wished to spend the day with you, and confess to a slight misrepresentation. But only slight. You have far more knowledge than I."

As he spoke, he drew her into an eight-sided inner chamber. Fallon caught her breath at the play of gaslight on an erotic marble coupling on a pedestal in the center of the room.

"Oh my," she breathed, her arm falling from Bridge's as she moved reverently toward the piece.

"A fan of sculpture, are you?" Bridge said. "I would have thought painting more your medium."

"I adore sculpture," Fallon said. "I wouldn't presume to think I could accomplish anything with a chunk of stone and some sharp tools, but I revere those who have the gift."

She reached toward the piece, then hesitated.

"One thing I learned at any early age is that sculpture is

meant to be appreciated by all the senses, not merely sight." He caught her hand in his and raised it up to his lips. Their gazes locked.

"Close your eyes," Bridge ordered as he bit down gently and proceeded to slowly, sensually, tug her fingers from their gloved prison, one digit at a time.

Fallon complied and felt herself sway toward him, drawn close as if controlled by a magnetic force stronger than her own limbs. She could feel the heat of his breath through the fabric of her glove, and the coolness of the room as her hand was exposed. How could she possibly be so hot and so cold at the same time?

"That's right," Bridge said. His voice sounded more resonant than usual, or perhaps it was just the echo in the high-ceilinged room. The sound of it lifted the hairs on the back of her neck, and she shivered as his hand guided hers to his lips. The tip of his tongue touched her palm, lightly at first, tracing tiny, erotic circles. The sensation radiated straight through her. From her scalp to the soles of her feet, she was awash in sensation.

"Sweet Fallon. Trusting Fallon." His voice was the slightest whisper in her ear.

She *did* trust him. Didn't she? Trust him how? To never lie? To never cheat? To never hurt her? She inhaled sharply. This was all wrong. These were the types of thoughts one harbored about a potential mate. She and Bridge were merely spending a final few hours together, no lifetimes. No commitment. No happily ever after. But she did love him, and love demanded trust. So he was right. He had won her trust. Together with her heart.

He guided her bare hand to the sculpture, cupped her compliant fingers around the cold marble.

"Tell me what you feel."

"It's smooth," Fallon said. "Cold as death. Which seems wrong when I know how alive it looks."

"To the eye it appears alive. The other senses know different."

Fallon took a sniff. "It has no scent."

"Actually, you're mistaken. Different stoneworks carry different and very distinct scents. But they're extremely subtle. It takes a lot of practice to discern, never mind to differentiate."

"All I can smell is you," Fallon confessed. "I would know your scent anyplace."

"As I would know yours."

She felt Bridge lean into her and draw a deep breath, then he exhaled hotly against the back of her neck. She shivered.

"Montague. I thought that was you, then wondered if my eyes had deceived me."

Fallon's eyes flew open in shock at the sound of a sharp, female voice. She turned and saw a tall, angular, black-garbed woman. And while the woman's words were directed at Bridge, her eyes were pinned upon Fallon, who felt herself shrinking beneath the pointed gaze.

To her dismay, Bridge abandoned her and approached the older woman, who turned one cheek in his direction. Bridge obviously knew his cue. He kissed the proffered cheek and drew her forward.

"Mother, what a delight to run into you here. I've someone I'd like you to meet. Fallon Gilchrist, my mother."

"How—how do you do, Mrs. Bridgeman," Fallon managed, beyond dismayed that the woman had seen the sensual way she'd been leaning against Bridge as she'd fondled the nude, erotic sculpture.

"Captain Gilchrist's widow?"

Fallon nodded silently. Standing beside the woman in her somber black ensemble, Fallon felt as cheap and showy as a whore in her ruby gown. She fought the urge to pull the edges of her cloak together. Why, oh why, had she let Bridge talk her into wearing the impossible frock?

"Your taste is improving, son. She's not your usual strumpet." The woman returned her attention to Fallon. "I was given to understand you had sequestered yourself on your late husband's estate. What brings you to our fair city?"

"Mother, you underestimate my powers of charm and persuasion." As Bridge looped a possessive arm across her shoulders, Fallon felt herself flush nearly as deep-hued as her gown.

"Montague, I have learned over the years to *never* underestimate you. Kindly allow Mrs. Gilchrist to speak for herself." She leveled a look toward Fallon.

Never one to back down from a challenge, Fallon drew herself as erect as possible, head high, shoulders straight. "Following my husband's death, I seemed to lose heart for my own art. Your son did indeed convince me I might rediscover my inspiration by viewing some of the exhibits in the Athenaeum. And, he insisted upon accompanying me to ensure I really made the trip."

The look in Mrs. Bridgeman's eyes, as they moved from

Fallon to Bridge and back, told Fallon that she wasn't fooled, not even for a minute.

"Montague is very much his father's son. A master at achieving his own ends."

"It was by your example I learned such tenacity," Bridge corrected. "Father was seldom around."

"He was around often enough to demonstrate several of his less desirable traits. Although I must say, your father's taste ran to women many years younger than himself. I shan't keep you two any longer. I have a committee meeting which requires my presence."

The old lady swept away, very much like a majestic raven. Even after the sound of her footsteps faded, her presence lingered, a cloyingly sweet perfume laden with an air of disapproval.

"Don't look so stricken," Bridge said, his fingers beneath Fallon's chin in a light caress. "Her bark is far worse than her bite."

"Easy for you to say. It wasn't you from whom she was drawing blood; it was I." Fallon's hands were shaking so badly she could hardly draw on her gloves. Bridge helped her with the simple task, keeping hold of both her hands in his afterward. He seemed so sure, so unflappable.

Fallon pulled away. *His* reputation was hardly at risk; it was already notorious. But what damage might befall hers?

"You're taking this little encounter far too seriously, my dear."

"Am I really?" Fallon asked. "Should I not be distressed to be labeled one of your strumpets?"

"Mother embraces a somewhat old-fashioned view of the world."

"Indeed? Her view is echoed by most of the population, when it comes right down to it."

"You really are upset. Do you wish to leave?"

"I do," Fallon said.

"Right, then," Bridge said. "Your wish is, as always, my command."

Fallon fell silent as they left the Athenaeum. She didn't want her wish to be Bridge's command. She hadn't asked for her life to be turned inside out, or her reputation to be in tatters. For a mature older woman such as herself to be seen in the company of a young man like Bridge . . . How ridiculous she must look, and rightly so. After all, her escort had been bought and paid for. How could she forget such a detail? It was her own fault that she'd been unmasked in all her folly, and ridiculed.

In the carriage she sat as far away from Bridge as possible, staring sightlessly out the window. The city, which only a few hours earlier had seemed so intriguing and full of life, now struck her as cold and dirty and unfriendly. She couldn't wait to flee to her sanctuary, back to the safety of her anonymity in the country.

She started when the carriage lurched to a stop. "Why are we stopping? I asked to go home."

"Earlier, you agreed to spend the day doing what I wish."

"I've changed my mind." She knew she sounded like a sulky child, but she didn't care a fig.

"Fallon," Bridge responded in tones one would use with a

querulous young person. "It's a lengthy journey back. We need to stop and have something to eat and refresh ourselves, first."

"I don't want to."

"Well, I do. You may feel free to sit in the carriage, if you wish." He started to leave, then turned back to face her. "Look at us. How ridiculous. We're adults."

"I am, at any rate. And quite capable of making my own decisions."

"Have it your way." Bridge swung out of the carriage and strode across the park. Fallon remained inside, suddenly unsure of what to do next. Sit there like a sulky child and await his return? Or order the driver to return to the country, leaving Bridge to his own devices?

She opened her mouth to issue the order, then stopped. This was not how she wished their last day together to end, without even a proper goodbye. Surely Bridge would feel the same? Surely he'd return any minute and coax her to join him? Eventually, she would relent. Reluctantly, of course, but graciously, nonetheless.

Fallon was glad she had no clock in front of her, for surely the minutes would tick by loudly, in painful slowness. She popped her head out the carriage window. No sign of Bridge. Finally, when she could sit still no longer, she opened the door and stepped out of the conveyance, wondering which direction Bridge had taken.

She was glancing about uncertainly and had just decided to ask the driver if he'd taken note of which direction Mr. Bridgeman had gone, when she heard, "Boo!"

Bridge popped up around the corner of the carriage.

Fallon jumped. "You startled me."

"Exactly my intention, my dear." He pulled out his time-piece. "You had exactly three more minutes before I planned to drag you out by the hair."

She managed a half smile. "I did want to see the park. And I will admit to being a bit peckish."

"I know the ideal picnic spot, where we can have our repast in complete privacy. Please do me the honor of joining me."

"Mrs. Buttle *would* be sorely miffed if her basket came back untouched."

"And we mustn't annoy Mrs. Buttle." Bridge fetched their picnic and offered Fallon his free arm.

It came as no great surprise that he would know the perfect location in the park for a private tryst. No doubt he was familiar with every secluded nook and cranny the city had to offer, availing himself of each and every opportunity to deflower a maiden, cuckhold a neglectful husband, or bring a slumbering widow back to life, the way he had done with her. How many other grateful women had found themselves on the receiving end of Bridge's carnal skills? How many women did it take to elevate one's lovemaking abilities to the master-ful level of Bridge's? She was but one in a long and unending line, a fact she would do well to remember.

The picnic site to which he led her was a cool, shaded nook, where a canopy of weeping branches and leaves shielded them from the view. A tiny stream gurgled past, no doubt leading to the lagoon. Light and shadow played upon the rich tones of the carriage blanket Bridge spread upon the thick, verdant grass. Fallon glanced up to see tantalizing glimpses of blue sky and sunshine peeking through nature's ceiling. A rich soil dampness spiked the air, the air rife with sunshine and floral scents.

The setting brought to mind the time they had made love outside in the rain. The time they had made love on the rose petals. She sighed. Would everything she saw continue to remind her in some way of intimate moments spent with Bridge?

"What was that sigh for?"

"I was just wondering . . ."

"Wondering what?" Bridge deposited the basket upon the lap robe, and removed his jacket.

"I was wondering how many women you've been with. How many you've been intimate with in this very spot."

"I make it a point never to revisit the past," Bridge said. "The future holds so much more to interest me."

"A lot of women, I take it."

"A lot," Bridge agreed.

"So many you've lost count."

"I've never attempted to keep count."

"I see," Fallon said.

"Now that I've satisfied your curiosity to the best of my abilities, come and have something to eat."

Fallon settled herself upon the lap rug and allowed Bridge to fill a plate for her with roast chicken, sweet pickles, and homemade bread.

"Mrs. Buttle forgot the most important picnic accompaniment," Bridge said, digging through the basket and coming up empty-handed.

"What's that?" Fallon asked.

"A good bottle of wine."

"I'm quite sure Mrs. Buttle disapproves of drink in the daylight hours."

"I'm quite certain that good woman disapproves of a lot of things, including me."

"I doubt my housekeeper's opinion of you holds much importance."

"I'm used to winning people's regard."

Yes, Bridge must be quite accustomed to swaying people his way. "Sometimes it takes more than a smile and a charming compliment to earn another's favor."

He slapped his knee. "Dash it, then; I'm ruined. For 'tis how I've learned to get by."

Fallon bit back a giggle. "Are you ever serious?"

"Good lord, no. Whatever for? I leave that to the stuffed shirts and the politicians."

"Politics," Fallon mused. "The ideal career choice. Should you ever decide to pursue a career, that is."

"I'll make you a deal. The day you apply yourself diligently to your art, take a risk, and mount a showing, that's the day I'll pursue something serious and important."

"That's hardly fair," Fallon protested. "Besides . . ."

"Besides?"

"After today, we'll never see each other again. We'll not know what the other one is about. Hence, I believe your idle days are guaranteed."

"Nothing," Bridge said, "is ever guaranteed." He leaned forward, plucked a piece of tender breast meat from her plate, and held it up to her lips.

Fallon hesitated, then opened her mouth, accepting the morsel from his fingers. The last meal they would share. The last time his fingers would linger against her lips. *No regrets,* she told herself staunchly. *Seize this moment and remember it.* So why did she suddenly find it so hard to swallow?

She was still struggling with her first bite when they were interrupted by the arrival of another couple, a young man and woman holding hands and laughing a secret laugh. The couple stopped short, their laughter dying. Tense silence reigned supreme, but only briefly.

"Bridge," said the dark-haired beauty. "Well, well. And here you'd led me to believe this was our special place."

"The whereabouts of which, you seem inclined to share as much as I," Bridge said.

"I grew used to sharing you. I believe you know Beau." She indicated the young man with his arm about her waist.

Bridge acknowledged the youth with a nod.

"And this must be the woman everyone's talking about. The one who paid handsomely for your services. She turned to Fallon in mock innocence. "Has Bridge given you your money's worth?"

Chapter Eleven

Mortified, Fallon dropped her plate, pushed herself to her feet, and plunged headlong through the leafy curtains and out into the park. She heard Bridge's footfalls behind her as she raced pell-mell toward her carriage. Strands of her hair pulled free as she ran, and blew wildly around her face, but she didn't care a fig about the odd looks being sent her way.

She knew Bridge was on her heels, just as she knew she had little hope of outrunning him. So why even try? Her wretched ruby frock left no room even to draw a deep breath. She slowed to a walk and tried to catch her breath. The little sprint had left her quite winded.

"Fallon." Bridge slowed with her, caught her arm, and turned her to face him. "Where are you tearing off to like that?"

"It's been a most enlightening week, Bridge. And an even more enlightening little jaunt into town. You've fulfilled your obligation, as I have fulfilled mine. I'm going back to the country."

"What's happened to upset you so?"

Fallon gave him a long, searching look and decided, *Yes, men truly are dense creatures.* "Your mother has labeled me a strumpet. Your friends have mocked me to my face. I think that counts as more than enough insults for one outing, wouldn't you?"

"Who cares what other people think?"

"Generally, Bridge, I do. I know you enjoy flauting society's rules and mores, and relish shocking people with your behavior. I don't. I do what's expected; I like the rules. I like knowing them and following them."

"Playing it safe," Bridge said.

"Some of us need to feel safe."

"So what's unsafe about being here with me today?"

Fallon sighed. Somehow she'd known that Bridge would not make it easy for her to leave. Even as she faced him she felt pangs of regret, a whisper of longing for what would never be.

She laid a gloved hand against his jaw. "Dear Bridge. This has been a week out of a dream, but the dream is over. Reality harkens."

"Describe your reality."

"My reality is that I am a middle-aged widow who must live her life quietly and modestly, as dictated by society. Not dash about town in the company of a handsome young rake, however charming and persuasive he might be."

Bridge set his lips in a stubborn frown. "You are saying we are taboo."

"You and I as a couple are very much taboo. And if I needed further convincing, today's excursion provided it."

Bridge linked his fingers through hers with fierce possessiveness and drew her against him. "I make you happy. I know I do."

"Your presence this past week has rendered me very happy indeed; beyond my wildest imaginings. But the censure we would receive, were we to keep further company, would destroy those happy memories and ultimately destroy everything good we had together."

"You're worried about the Boston set. We can leave. There are dozens of other cities where we could be happy, where the people are not so backward in their thinking. Paris. Rome. London."

Fallon smiled sadly and stepped back from him. "You make it sound very tempting. And perhaps for a while, we could be happy someplace else. But eventually one or both of us would miss our roots and want to come back here, only to find that nothing has changed."

"We could change."

"Bridge, my dear, I'm too old to change. And I would hate for you to attempt to change who you are. Even for me."

She wasn't certain she had convinced him until he said, "I'll see you home."

"No, my love. We'll say goodbye here and now. It truly was a week out of time and I shall never forget it."

Bridge looked as if he had other things he wished to say, but he pressed his lips tightly together. He handed her into the carriage, slammed the door louder than necessary, turned, and walked away.

"So, was he as divine as he looks?"

Fallon all but unseated herself at the unexpected sight and sound of her friend. "Anna! What on earth are you doing here?"

"Getting a firsthand accounting of my gift, of course. What else?"

"You scared me half to death. I meant, how did you come to be sitting in my carriage?"

"I was driving through the park when I recognized your carriage and saw you running across the green, with young Bridgeman at your heels. I simply popped into your carriage and dismissed mine. You can drop me at my home on your way. Now, tell Auntie Anna everything." She gave a comfortable wiggle as she settled back in her seat.

"I don't suppose it would occur to you that some things might be too private to share?"

"Oh ho!" Following her most unladylike hoot of delight, Anna leaned forward and gave Fallon a fierce, quick hug. "I have my old friend back."

"Indeed," Fallon murmured. "I'm painting better than ever, you'll be most happy to hear."

"You're blushing," Anna crowed triumphantly. "I knew it. Young Bridgeman inspired you in all manner of ways, did he not?"

"You might say that. How young *is* he? I never did find out."

"Not all that young. Twenty-four to your twenty-nine, I believe. At any rate, why so glum? Why the bittersweet farewell?"

"The week is over. We return to our lives. He to his wastrel ways and I to my studio."

"No talk of continuing to . . ." Anna paused as if searching for the right words. "To spend time together in the future?"

"No," Fallon said, settling back and crossing her arms over her chest with an air of finality. "It's done."

Anna linked her arm through Fallon's. "All's well that ends well. Isn't that what they say?"

"Something like that," Fallon said hollowly.

She declined Anna's plea to stop in for tea, citing exhaustion and a long drive ahead of her. When she finally reached the estate, she ordered a hot bath, refused supper, and fell into an exhausted yet restless sleep.

She awoke early, but rather than the listless torpor that had plagued her since her husband's demise, she felt herself overflowing with creative energy. The household had yet to stir as she made her way to her studio.

The first thing that met her eyes upon entering was Bridge's portrait. Artistic prejudices aside, she knew it was her best work ever. Her subject appeared alive, as if he could rise off the canvas and take her into his arms.

She shivered, so real was his presence. And she longed for him. To feel his skin against her skin, his breath upon her brow, his lips claiming hers. The contagious rumble of his low masculine chuckle when he found something amusing. And Bridge found much to laugh about. He'd brought laughter back into her life. Laughter and love.

Fortunately, missing him was a dull ache rather than a debilitating pain. Surely time, coupled with keeping herself busy, would diminish the ache until it, along with Bridge, was naught but a cloudy memory.

She picked up a brush, put it down, then picked it up again, flicking the dry bristles across the palm of her hand. Tingles of awareness chased the length of her arm. Would she ever again be able to gaze upon a paintbrush and not recall the way Bridge had employed one as an erotic stimulation for their lovemaking?

She wandered about the studio, touching the settee where he had posed, the table where he had eaten, the floor where they had made love. She even found a few dried rose petals, forgotten in the far corner of the room. Sentimentally she raised them to her nose, but their fragrance was long gone.

"The bloom has definitely left the rose, my dear." She spoke aloud, her voice echoing hollowly in the studio. Then she positioned a blank, primed canvas on her easel, squeezed colors from their tubes onto her palette, and started to paint.

She worked in an energetic frenzy where days merged into weeks. Fortunately the days were at their zenith as the summer solstice approached, the daylight hours lengthy, the long stretch of sunlight every day ideal for her work.

"'Tisn't right, madam," Mrs. Buttle scolded her one day as she exchanged one nearly untouched tray of food for a fresh one. "There's more to life than painting."

"I know you're correct, Mrs. Buttle. But right now, I feel I simply must strike while the iron is hot." She laid aside her brush and walked the housekeeper to the door, as if to convince the woman that she was not totally possessed. "Really, I appreciate your preparing all my favorite foods."

"You're fair wasting away," Mrs. Buttle said chastisingly.

"I'm eating plenty. Sleeping better than I ever have. And I'm happy. Please don't fret."

"Hmmph," was the housekeeper's only parting remark. The food untouched, Fallon hastened back to her painting. Across the room, from its place of honor, Bridge's likeness watched her. She could sense his support and approval, understanding as no one else ever could the passion that drove her.

Truly, Bridge had understood many things about her that no one else ever had or ever would. She allowed herself a tantalizing game of "what if." What if their ages and stations were more closely suited? What if he took a fancy to settle down? What if he arrived one day, hat in hand, a declation of undying love on his lips?

You're too old to believe in fairy tales, my dear. Face it, where Bridge is concerned, you are out of sight and most assuredly out of mind.

Fallon celebrated the summer solstice alone in her garden beneath the full moon. She knew she would need to hurry to finish the series she was working on. Each day the sun would set a little earlier and rise a little later, shortening her hours of natural light.

～　～　～

THE FULL MOON found its way through the partially drawn curtains to the rumpled and messy bed where Bridge lay, unable to sleep. He'd already sent his companion for the evening home some hours earlier. He no longer took the same delight from fresh conquests. In fact, he'd gone through the motions this evening with a haste previously unknown to him. He wanted only to get the act over with and the young woman sent on her way. Yet now, he found himself alone and unable to sleep.

He'd driven around the countryside on several occasions, but was unsuccessful in his attempt to locate Fallon Gilchrist's estate. He prided himself on having a good sense of direction, so each fruitless search left him more surly and frustrated than the last.

He'd been blindfolded when he was first taken there, and too damn distracted giving Fallon oral pleasure on the trip to the city to have any clue as to where he had spent the week in between. He had hunted down her friend Anna, who had flatly refused to divulge Fallon's whereabouts. He had even asked his mother if she chanced to know the location of the Gilchrist country estate. But Mother and her friends knew only of the Gilchrist townhouse, and when he stopped by there he found it rented to a family of foreigners, who, if they had knowledge of Fallon's whereabouts, were keeping it to themselves.

His friends had given him up for the bad company he knew he was. He had tried losing himself in drink, but it seemed the more he drank the more sober he became. Gaming and whoring held no appeal. Nor did the rounds of polite society.

"Damn moonlight." Bridge rolled over and punched his pillow. Yet all he could think about was the way the moonlight spilled through the studio windows; the way it shimmered on Fallon's alabaster limbs, and shadowed the delicious triangle between her thighs.

How on earth could he hope to convince her that they belonged together, if he couldn't even find her?

Chapter Twelve

"*I hear young Bridgeman* is a mess," Anna began conversationally as she sipped from her delicate Spode teacup.

"Mmmmmm." On the other side of the studio, half hidden behind her canvas, Fallon frowned at her latest endeavor, giving her friend barely half of her attention.

"Fallon. Did you hear what I said?"

"What? Of course."

"Very well, then. What did I say?"

With a weighty sigh, Fallon laid down her palette and brush and rounded her easel. "Caught in a lie. I didn't hear what you said."

"I knew that," Anna said smugly. "For my remark quite warranted more than a murmur in response. I said, our friend Bridgeman is reputed to be in a sorry state. Drinking and gaming and whoring like a man with nothing left to live for."

"That's a shame," Fallon said, trying not to let on how the thought of Bridge with other women punctured a hole in her heart. "He has so much intelligence and potential."

"And how is the painting progressing?" Anna said, changing the subject before Fallon was ready to have it changed.

"I fear I have lost whatever momentum was charging my efforts these past weeks," Fallon said. "At this rate, I'll never be ready."

"You must!" Anna sounded truly aghast. "You have everything riding on this. You won't be granted a second chance to exhibit at the Athenaeum."

"I'm aware of that fact," Fallon replied crossly. She was afraid—no, she was more than afraid—that her waning creativity was due to Bridge's absence. For as time passed, so did her inspiration and her talent, eventually drying up till there was nothing left.

"There must be something you can do about it," Anna insisted. "Some source of inspiration you can tap in to."

"Bridgeman," Fallon said mockingly.

"That's it!" Anna leaped to her feet and clapped her hands together.

"What's it, darling? Are you daft? Sit down and finish your tea."

"No," Anna said, "listen. I have the most perfect scheme."

"You and your schemes. Are there no end to the devious plots in that blonde head of yours?"

"There was not one thing wrong with my last outrageous idea. And this is a natural one with which to follow."

Normally Fallon would have dismissed Anna's outlandish scheme out of hand directly. But times were no longer normal. She was duty-bound, not simply for her own sake but for the sake of Boston's growing legion of women artists, to ensure the success of her upcoming exhibition.

If one more night in Bridge's company could refill her creative well, then that was a sacrifice she had no choice but to make. For the sake of women artists everywhere, of course.

BRIDGE AWOKE to a ruckus of raised voices downstairs in his townhouse, and swore to himself impatiently. Damn it, he had left explicit instructions that he was *not* to be disturbed, no matter what, not even if the damn city was burning down around him.

The commotion grew louder and seemed to be headed his way, clattering up the stairs to his room. Groggily, Bridge slung his legs over the side of his bed and tried to think. How long since he'd had a decent sleep? How long since his dreams hadn't been plagued by memories of Fallon? Some nights he swore he could smell her in the room with him, hear her laughter taunting him. He hated that a mere woman had sent his life into such turmoil.

He was still sitting on the side of the bed with his head in his hands when the door burst open.

"Bloody hell!" he thundered. "Does no one around here

understand the meaning of not disturbing me under any circumstances?"

"My, my. Aren't you a sorry sight."

He glanced up through eyes heavy with fatigue. "Hello, Mother."

"Are you ill?"

Bridge managed a hollow laugh. *Sick at heart, perhaps. But hardly physically ill.* "I'm quite well, thank you."

His mother advanced into the room and wrinkled her nose at the smell. "You don't appear to be quite well. You look more of a mess than I ever recall seeing you, and I've witnessed you in some sorry states."

"Don't remind me," Bridge said.

"I suppose you're going to say this time is different."

"How would you know that?"

"Because I've witnessed the change. You've been busy and productive. You've found a cause you believe in. Or have you forgotten?"

"I've forgotten nothing. I've had a temporary relapse, is all. I'll be back in stride forthwith."

"That's reassuring to hear. I've taken the liberty of ordering you a bath."

"That's a pretty big liberty. Even for you."

"I have the feeling you won't hold it against me."

As soon as his mother left, his bath arrived and he eased into the steaming water. It was true, he'd been enjoying his patronage of the Massachusetts Normal Art School. Not only did being around artists make him feel somehow closer to Fallon, it was also a cause he believed in. Activity, a feeling of accomplishment . . . these were not new to him, but this felt more fulfilling than anything he'd tackled previously.

"Dash it all. Can't a man get a little help around his own home?" Bridge bellowed.

Behind him, he heard the door to his bedchamber open, felt the whisper of a draft across his damp skin. "It's about time. Close the door, man. Do you want me to catch my death?" The flame of the candle near the washtub flickered as the door closed with a muffled click.

Bridge sat forward in the tub as footfalls rounded the screen behind him. "Wash my back, and be quick about it. The water grows chill and I'm turning into a prune waiting."

He closed his eyes and gave a heartfelt sigh of pleasure as the abrasive flannel sleeked across his bare back and shoulders. There was something infinitely soothing about the circular motion, the pressure of another's touch upon his bare skin.

Mercy. Now he was finding his valet's touch inciting. He did need to pull himself together.

"Watch it, Max. Not so rough," he said as the flannel scraped the back of his neck.

"That's enough." He batted Max away and leaned back against the washtub, but not before he realized that something was different. Max did not wear lace cuffs. He grasped the newcomer's wrist and turned around.

"Fallon!" He blinked. So many times, he had brought her image to mind—was this one of those illusions, come to haunt him? Did he perchance dream instead of wake?

Yet in his dreams she was never dressed as she was now in the uniform of a maid. "What game do you play?"

"You asked me once what I thought would happen were you to own me, rather than the other way round. I thought it would be amusing to see."

"That's what I've become to you? A source of amusement?"

"On the contrary," Fallon said softly, "you became the source of inspiration for my art."

"And now?"

"And now I am yours to command, as you will, till the sun once more appears upon the horizon."

"Bloody hell!" Bridge thundered. "Get naked and get in here with me."

A faint smile touched her lips. "Your wish is my command, O master."

"Disrobe slowly," Bridge ordered. "I wish to savor the anticipation."

"Yet you doffed your clothing so quickly, when you were mine to command."

"Perhaps my half-fortnight with you has taught me patience."

"I don't believe patience is inherent in your nature." As she spoke, she removed the maid's cap, which masked her glorious hair.

"Let your hair down," Bridge commanded. "I wish to see the candlelight capture its essence."

One by one, she removed the pins and dropped them at her feet. Bridge licked his lips as he watched her. Now he knew how a starving man must feel when led to a fully laden table. Strand by strand, her hair tumbled down about her shoulders like pale spun gold. He itched to touch its silken threads, to raise it to his nostrils, to drown in the special smell of her. His breath caught as she shook her head and tumbled the mane so it clung to her bosom, cruelly camouflaged as outlined in the starched black primness of the uniform.

"Better?" she asked seductively.

Bridge exhaled on a ragged sigh. "Much."

Slowly she unbuttoned her cuffs, affording him a glimpse of delicate pale wrists. Reaching behind, she untied her apron and allowed it to flutter to her feet.

"Umm-hmm," Bridge said approvingly. Very deliberately he grasped the bar of soap and began sliding it across his torso in a slow, sensual manner. His movements clearly caught her interest; he saw her eyes widen appreciatively. Her fingers fumbled ever so slightly as she began to unfasten the buttons on the stiff black damask of her uniform.

"Tease me," Bridge ordered as the snowy white of her chemise winked at him from beneath the black gown.

"I beg your pardon?"

"Tease me," Bridge repeated. "You are, after all, mine to command. Is that not so?"

As he spoke he continued to glide the soap across his skin, well aware that Fallon's excitement grew to match his own. Why else would she possibly be here?

She finished undoing all the buttons, then paused. Bridge could hardly wait to see what she would do next.

She reached inside the frock and ran her hands lovingly across her bosom, her ribs, her waist, outlining her shape.

Emphasizing the difference between her hourglass softness and his masculine form. When she gave a slight shrug of her shoulders, the frock slid from her body and pooled at her feet. She kicked it aside as she neared the washtub. He waited. She scooped up a handful of water and dampened the front of her chemise, rendering the thin lawn fabric nearly transparent. He could clearly see her nipples, proudly pebbled into tight buds in the centers of her darker areolas. Using only the middle finger of each hand she massaged her nipples, then dragged her nails across their tightly engorged surfaces. He swore he could hear the rasp of fingernail against fabric. Eyes half closed, head thrown back, she clearly showed him how much she was enjoying their game.

"Does that feel good?" Bridge prompted.

"Very." The one word answer was drawn slowly, like the purr of a contented feline.

"Where else are you wet?"

Her hands roamed across her torso to settle at the juncture of her thighs.

"Here." She parted her legs slightly.

Bridge caught his breath at the shadowy triangle revealed by her movement.

"Come here," he commanded.

Her hips swayed from side to side as she made her way toward him.

"Now put one foot atop the side of the washtub."

She did as he bade her, revealing a most interesting alteration to her undergarments.

"I can't quite see," he said pleasantly. "Please help me out."

"Certainly, master." She put a hand on each thigh and drew them apart, revealing her innermost bounty, moist and pink and utterly delicious.

"You naughty girl," he said. "It appears you've ripped your knickers."

As he spoke, he slipped his hand between her thighs and stroked the soft white skin that tempted him, before burrowing deeper and lightly sleeking the soft, pouty lips of her femininity.

She gave a half sigh, half murmur of approval.

"There are scissors on the nightstand," he said abruptly. "Fetch them."

"Yes, master." Removing her foot from its perch, Fallon turned and sashayed away, an exaggerated swing to her hips. He enjoyed watching the way the fabric pulled across the lush fullness of her curves.

He was harder than he'd ever been in his life, yet he had no intention of rushing the pleasure he knew awaited them both.

She returned with the scissors and passed them to him, handle first.

"Now lean close."

Very carefully he tucked his free hand down the front of her chemise, fingers guiding the pathway of the scissors as he cut out a small piece from each side, just large enough for her nipples to poke through.

She glanced down at herself. "Now look what you've done. Fair ruined my undergarments."

"Let's think of it more as 'enhanced' your undergarments, my dear." He stood, lifted her up, and brought her into the tub alongside him.

"Oh," she said. "Now my stockings are all wet."

"Indeed," he agreed pleasantly. "Allow me to remove them for you." Reaching beneath the ruffle edging her pantalets, he rolled down her stocking. She balanced by holding on to his shoulder as she obediently lifted first one foot, then its mate. Soggy stockings joined her discarded dress.

"I do believe you're in need of a wash." Bridge brought up the soap between them and made a point of thoroughly soaping her exposed nipples. She made a low, approving noise far back in her throat. Water dripped down across her ribs to her waist, dampening the front of her chemise and revealing the soft pink skin beneath.

Then Bridge settled her on the rim of the tub, pushed her knees wide apart, and knelt between them. He paused, looking his fill. Had he ever even dreamed of a sight so exciting as Fallon, in half-damp underpinnings? The provocative hide-and-seek peek-a-boo of her nipples and her pussy, coupled with her bare legs and ankles, was a powerful enticement. He placed his hands on her knees and buried his face between her legs. She gasped at the first touch of his lips to her flesh, then shuddered as his talented tongue found the hidden pearl of her woman's pleasure. It danced beneath his ministrations, grew harder and more engorged with excitement, like the tiniest of penises. Her juices filled his mouth with ecstasy as he twined the tiny nub, his tongue lashing it with dizzying swirls, until with a final, gentle suck, he felt her release.

Heard her scream of triumph as her entire body shuddered and finally grew still.

He sat back in the tub, the water long grown cool, and pulled her down with him so she was settled on his lap. "What else happens to ladies who rip their knickers?" he inquired pleasantly.

"Nothing until you kiss me," Fallon said. "I die for your kisses."

"And I die for your pussy."

She pushed out her lower lip in a mock pout. "The water is cold."

"So it is. I am a very bad host." He rose and steadied her as she stepped from the tub. "Let's get you out of those wet things," he said, tossing a towel in her direction.

He dried himself quickly, then helped her peel the ruined undergarments from her body. Gooseflesh pebbled her skin. "You're cold," he said. "Come sit by the fire and I'll pour you a brandy."

He tugged a covering from his bed and wrapped it about her shoulders. Then he placed a snifter of brandy in her hand.

"Now then," he said. "Now that you've had your fun and games, what exactly are you doing here? How did you even know where to find me?"

"One with your reputation can hardly remain incognito, Bridge. Even in a city the size of Boston."

"I see. Well, I believe you said you're mine for the night." He waved a hand toward the bed. "I expect you there when I return."

"When you return?"

He rose and began to dress. "When I return. For you see, I have an engagement this evening. And just because it suits you to appear on my doorstep in a trollopy mood doesn't mean it suits me, as well."

Fallon pressed her lips together tightly and appeared to hunch down beneath her lone cover. "I didn't mean to be presumptuous."

"But you were." Bridge finished dressing and left her sitting by the fire.

Fallon finished her brandy in solitary misery. Part of her longed to flee back to the country. Bridge in the city was a far cry from the Bridge she'd painted in her studio. But she also knew that this was part of a test. Bridge expected her to flee, as the Fallon of old would have. But she'd promised him herself until the sun tinged the horizon, and she determined to remain with or without his presence.

She refilled her empty brandy glass, feeling its burning warmth chase all the way to her inner organs, a sad second place to the heat Bridge kindled inside her. But the brandy made her feel less lonely and she topped her glass a third time, and then a fourth.

Bridge had made his point very well, she conceded as she climbed into his bed, her eyes far too heavy to remain open. She'd shown up professing subservience, yet still had presumed to be holding the reins. While this new version of Bridge was different, stronger, more in control, she couldn't help but feel she preferred him this way. She'd been expecting to find him moping about, drinking too much, and generally acting a lilyliver, when the exact opposite was true.

Later, something disturbed her dreams and eventually pulled her from the warm safety of sleep. She stirred and tried to turn and stretch, only to find her movements severely restricted. When she opened her eyes, all stayed black. She was blindfolded, she realized with a start of fear. Her hands and feet were bound, not together, but secured apart, toward the bedposts.

"Bridge," she said. His name came out a frightened croak. "Bridge, I'm afraid." Dear Lord, let it be Bridge who had rendered her thus, and not some maniacal madman.

"I'm here, my dear. No need to be frightened."

"Please untie me. I don't like feeling this way."

She felt the mattress dip beneath his weight as he joined her.

"And how do you feel?"

"Helpless," she said.

"Have you felt helpless before?"

She nodded. Of course she had. When her parents died. When her newborn infant struggled for breath, then gave up the struggle. When her husband's absence at sea stretched so long, she faced the fact that he would never return.

"What else do you equate with helplessness?"

"Loss." Her answer was automatic.

"So tonight, you shall have a new experience. Helpless perhaps, yet with nothing to lose. And everything to gain."

"Bridge, please untie me."

She felt him then, all of him, naked, stretched atop her. Kissing her the way she longed to be kissed. With passion, hunger, need, skill, love.

Not love, she told herself. Bridge didn't love her.

"Fallon, I promise you I would never hurt you. I shall untie you whenever you wish. But think carefully before you ask. Think if you are willing to take a chance. To learn that helplessness does not always follow loss. To accept that helplessness can simply be the means to allow someone else to take charge, just for a short time."

"Like you did with me at my studio," she said.

"Exactly the same. I have no desire to frighten you. But I do feel you came here tonight to experience something new, if only something you can carry back and explore in your paintings. A new depth of passion as, together, we explore waters yet uncharted. Are you with me? Or do I unbind you and send you on your way?"

Fallon was torn, poised between two worlds. Old and safe. New and exciting. The choice was hers.

"You're right," Fallon said. "I told you I was yours to do with as you wished, until the sun stained the horizon with tomorrow's dawn."

"Very good." He trailed his fingertips across her lips, outlining their shape, dampening his skin with her saliva.

"Am I allowed to taste you?" she asked.

"I am yours to sample."

As she sucked his fingertips, one at a time, she became aware of a soft tickling pressure across her abdomen and thighs.

"What is that?"

"Can you guess?"

"It's softer than your fingertips; they're quite callused."

"You're right. It's not my fingers."

"A bit of lace?"

"Afraid not."

"I know," she said triumphantly. "A feather."

"Not a feather, either."

The sensation continued. Across the sensitive crease at the top of her inner thighs. Over the jutting ridge of her hipbone, trailing across the concave line of her stomach before easing lower to her pubes. Her skin prickled and grew moist. She felt her vagina lips swell, her clit begin to pulse as she tried to imagine what Bridge used to stimulate her. Whatever it was, it grazed her labia lips, lighter than any lover's kiss.

"Do you give up?" Bridge asked. His stimulant had now found its way to the sensitive skin on the underside of her arms. From there it traversed to her breasts, circled round and around her nipples.

"It reminds me of the time you painted me with the dry brushes," she said. "But this is softer than the softest sable. May I smell?"

The object was whisked beneath her nose, across her upper lip.

"Not a rose," she announced in disappointment. "Nor any sort of flower."

"It is a hard one to guess."

"Give me more clues."

"It's something I carry on my person at all times."

"That's not a clue," Fallon said. "That's a red herring. Men don't carry soft things. . . . Wait. I know."

"Do you?"

"I believe so."

"Shall I remove the blindfold so you can see if you're right?"

"No. I trust you to tell me if I'm right."

"You trust me? That's good."

"I have to trust you. Otherwise this little game we play would terrify me."

"I would hate to terrify you."

She felt the mattress shift, knew he knelt above her, straddling her.

"I long to touch you, you know."

"All in good time." She could feel his erection brushing against her mons, seeking her inner heat. His fingers replaced his toy against her taut inner thighs.

"I'm waiting for your guess," he said with a throaty laugh. "You get rewarded if you're right. And punished if you guess wrong."

"It was a rabbit's foot," she said triumphantly.

He laughed. "You're good at this game."

"And what's my reward?"

He leaned forward and gently tweaked her nipples. She caught her breath at the instant rush of heightened sensations, fueling the damp, needful heat of her loins.

"Bridge," she said with a half gasp.

"Feels good, doesn't it? Your reward has just begun." He pinched her nipples with more vigor. "Tell me if I'm being too rough."

She rolled her head from side to side, longing to open her

legs wider, longing to feel him embedded inside of her, quenching the fiery need.

"More," she said. "I want more."

"You want me to pet your pussy?" he said. "Like this?" His clever fingers parted the outer lips and stroked the hot, wet softness within, studiously ignoring the pulsing nub of her clit.

She moaned.

"You're at my mercy, you know." His cock replaced his fingers, rooting around near the opening to her sex.

"Yes," she said.

"Tell me to fuck you."

"Fuck me," she begged. "Fuck me now. Fuck me hard."

She felt his smooth, slow entry and nearly sobbed in relief.

"Does that feel good inside you?"

"Oh, yes."

"In and out like this?"

Withdraw. Reenter. With maddening slowness that was effectively driving her crazy with need.

She panted, whimpered, moaned, chafing against her bonds. Uttering guttural sounds she didn't even recognize as belonging to her.

"I need to come. Lord, I shall go mad if I don't come."

"Indeed," he said pleasantly.

She felt him shifting positions even as the rhythmic penetration continued, then swelled as he slipped his pinkie finger inside her anus.

"Oh," she gasped.

"You like that more this time, I take it."

She was too overwhelmed with new sensations to answer. Gaining release paled in importance.

"Still want me to make you come?" he asked.

"No," she surprised herself by saying.

"Too bad."

She felt his hot breath against her mound, his talented tongue and lips finding her clitoris, and sucking in time to the in-out motion in her vagina and her anus.

Fallon screamed. She came and came and came again, so many times she lost count. Orgasm piled atop orgasm, a pleasure so intense it bordered on pain. And still he kept eating her. Licking, sucking, tasting, as if he would consume all of her and leave nothing but a shell. She was existing in a world where nothing mattered but sexual ecstasy of the most intense extremes.

Just when she thought she couldn't possibly climax again, she felt his penetration and rode a fresh wave of release.

He withdrew and lay alongside her, panting in rhythm with her. He reached across, removed her blindfold, and kissed her with a gnawing hunger.

"You're still hard," she said wonderingly, feeling him ramrod stiff against her.

"I am." He shifted about, untying her wrists and ankles. Freed from her bonds, she felt too limp to move.

"How can that be?"

"I haven't been in you yet."

"You haven't . . . What was . . . ?"

"A prop I make use of from time to time. Very lifelike, is it not?"

"May I see it?"

"Later," he said. "Right now I have need of you. Make love to me with your mouth."

"Your wish is my command."

She settled herself between his legs and took him slowly into her mouth. He groaned in pleasure and she grew more bold, moving her lips and her tongue in similar fashion to his actions with her earlier. She moistened her pinkie and slid it inside him as he had done to her, gratified to hear his deep, approving moan of pleasure.

Emboldened, she used it to pleasure him as her tongue and lips tortured his swollen member. She heard him panting, groaning; then his hands tangled in her hair and pulled hard as he exploded inside her mouth.

She swallowed convulsively, then turned him over and continued to lick and suckle his anus and balls. Within minutes, he grew hard again. She crawled across the bed, positioning herself before him, derriere in the air.

"Doggy-style, if you don't mind. I quite enjoy it that way."

"Whatever you say."

Still slick and wet, she felt him slide snugly inside her and begin pumping away with gusto. She reached between them to play with his balls and rub her clit. They came together in mutual ecstasy as, outside, the first rosy petals of dawn lightened the summer sky.

She rose almost immediately. Her turn to leave him, and she'd do it in style.

He rolled to face her. "Where are you going?"

It's sunrise. Your time with me is up.

"I gave you a full seven days and seven nights. Yet you're giving me only one night?"

"My gift to you, in exchange for yours to me. The renewal of my passion for my art."

"And what of our passion for each other?"

"I'm painting again, making something of my life. As you must make something of yours."

Chapter Thirteen

Bridge sat staring at the papers before him, unable to focus. Two weeks since that night Fallon had come to him, and nothing had been the same. He missed her with a consuming need that rendered him near useless in all other aspects of his life. For the first time since the war, he was consumed by fear. What if he approached her, only to suffer her rejection? Everything was at stake, his life, his future, rendering him nearly paralyzed. He was accustomed to pursuing what he wanted and devil take anyone who got in his way. But this time the stakes were too high. He had to make something of his life. Prove himself worthy of her.

There was a knock at his study door, followed by the appearance of his sister, Agatha. "Am I interrupting?"

"Happily." Bridge rose and gave his sister a hug. "Aggie, what brings you here?"

"I was concerned. My sources report you rarely leave the house, and haven't been seen around the college in weeks."

"My work with the college is done. I'm looking toward a new venture or two."

"That's good news. I was afraid your reclusion might be due to the fact that the entire town is talking about you and that Gilchrist woman and her painting of you."

"What?" Bridge gripped her shoulders urgently.

Agatha patted his hands. "I've just come from the Athenaeum. You would know what's going on, if you ever left your home."

"What about Fallon's painting?"

"Paintings. The Gilchrist woman has an entire exhibit at the Athenaeum, and is causing quite a stir with it."

Bridge released her. "How so?"

"Well, the series on display is unusual enough in itself. Particularly for a first exhibit. Striking, boldly dramatic—quite risky, actually. Not the usual boring still lifes or land-scapes so many artists paint."

"So she's changed her style," Bridge murmured, more to himself than to his sister.

"I wouldn't know about that. But I must say the entire town is agog over the portrait of you which she has included with her works."

"It's on exhibit as well? You've seen it?"

"I have. It's quite an interesting likeness. She's captured something. But then, I expect you know exactly what I'm talking about."

Bridge felt a flash of panic, then gave himself a mental shake. He had nothing to apologize for; he was old enough to decide when and where to pose in the nude. Still, he hadn't anticipated not only his family seeing him in all his naked splendor, but the entire city of Boston, from the sound of it.

"You liked the portrait?"

"It wouldn't be my choice of poses for a formal sitting, but I do like it, yes. Mother tried to purchase it from Mrs. Gilchrist, but she was very firm on its not being for sale. Not at any price."

"Mother tried to buy the portrait Fallon painted of me?"

"Face it, Montague. Despite the way you often act, you're not getting any younger. We all thought it would be a nice addition to the family portraits."

Bridge gave his head a shake and wondered about his hearing. His mother, attempting to purchase his nude portrait, and not to remove it from public scrutiny but as some sort of family legacy?

He rose to his feet. "It doesn't seem right that I'm the last person in town to see Fallon's exhibit."

"I thought you might feel that way. There is a reception this evening with the artist in attendance. Invitation only. Dress is formal." Agatha rummaged through her reticule. "I took the liberty of securing you an invitation."

Bridge crossed the room to give his sister a hug. "You are a most insightful and amazing woman."

"I know that. I admit to having had my doubts when I first heard about you with her. But as I thought about it afterwards, I drew the conclusion that an older, more mature woman is exactly the steady influence you would benefit most from."

"Hang the steady influence. I'm in love with the woman."

His sister shrugged. "That, my dear brother, is most pathetically obvious. And seeing you through her eyes, as she painted you, I would wager the feeling to be quite mutual."

Those words gave him courage as he made his way that evening through the crowded reception lobby of the Athenaeum. Party protocol seemed to have abandoned him. He had once been the master of effortless, mindless chatter with near strangers. Tonight, all he cared about was seeing Fallon.

He stopped a waiter who circled the room with a full tray of champagne, held the man's arm while he drained one glass in a single swallow, then exchanged it for a full one.

"Thank you, my good man," he said.

"Very good, sir." The waiter was a study in poker face, but Bridge sensed his disapproval. Once, such silent censure wouldn't have merited even a notice. When had he started caring what other people thought of him? When he had started caring what Fallon thought. Hers was the only opinion that mattered.

He made his way through the black-suited men and rainbow-hue-gowned women, and wondered what Fallon was wearing. Hopefully not black, still pretending to be in mourning. Was she was even there yet? And how would she feel when she saw him? He wondered how she had been since that memorable evening when she'd invaded his chamber, his very own fantasy come to life.

He paused at the base of the curving marble staircase and gripped the glossy white handrail. Her exhibit was on the second floor. His legs felt unbelievably heavy as he made the climb.

"Bridge, my man."

Bridge paused at the top of the stairs. Too late now; he'd been spotted by a former classmate. Naively, he'd hoped to make his way unnoticed to his portrait.

"Hello, Giles." The two men shook hands.

"I must say, you're looking in fine form. Not quite as comely as your likeness in the other room, but well, nonetheless. I take it you and the artist are, shall we say, intimately acquainted?"

In spite of himself, Bridge felt a slow heat creep up from under the tight collar of his formal shirt.

"We had several sittings," he said, carefully.

"So I should wager. Well, I won't keep you. See you at the club sometime soon?"

"I expect so."

The chamber showcasing Fallon's exhibit was even more crowded than the entrance lobby. Bridge sipped his champagne as he inspected Fallon's new work. The paintings were wild and earthy in their boldness. He could almost feel the pelting rain on his face in one. Another all but blinded him with the beauty of the sunset.

"Damn good, isn't she?" said a chap next to him.

"She always was, but in these, she has definitely found her own style," Bridge agreed.

"I tried to buy this one but I was too late. The entire show is sold out." The man looked at Bridge directly. "Say, you're the chap. *Still Man in Motion.*"

"I beg your pardon?"

"The painting. The one the artist refuses to sell. Fair likeness, I might add."

"Indeed." Bridge cleared his throat. He hadn't thought it would bother him, but the knowledge that every person in the room had seen him captured in an unclothed state was a trifle unsettling. "I should go have a gander. If you'll excuse me."

"But of course. It's over on the far wall."

With great trepidation, Bridge made his way through the room. He took a breath. This was it. The crowd parted. He faced his future . . . And froze in astonishment.

It was Fallon's likeness of him, and yet it was not. He laughed aloud, then stepped closer to inspect the piece more fully.

"You minx," he said admiringly under his breath.

For Fallon had painted him fully clothed. True, his shirt was unbuttoned, his chest partially revealed. He was wearing casual trousers and riding boots. He looked relaxed and happy, sprawled comfortably across the settee as if he'd just come in and flopped down before the woman he loved. And then he smelled her, the same scent that haunted his sleepless nights.

"Well, what do you think?"

He turned. She was real. All shimmery in an emerald evening gown, diamonds in her ears and circling her throat. He ached all over just from the sight of her. "I think the artist is the most amazingly talented woman I have ever met. As well as the most beautiful."

Fallon smiled, and the glow in her eyes transformed her face into a beacon. Bridge caught his breath. Could his sister be right? Could Fallon love him even half as much as he loved her?

"Not only are you a gifted artist, I must thank you for having saved my reputation."

"Truth be told, I wasn't entirely sure it was worth saving," Fallon murmured.

"I fully expected to find myself spread-eagled in all my naked glory for the devouring eyes of Boston to cackle over," he said.

"I'm sure many of the ladies present would have preferred the original version of the portrait."

"And the artist herself?"

Fallon cocked her head. "I'm not sure. There is something rather evocative in this one. One can't help but wonder how long it will be until someone comes along and peels your garments from your body. Perhaps I'll do a series. In the next one you shall be clad only in your trousers, your shirt a rumpled scrap of silk on the floor. And so on."

"Only if I get to pose."

"That won't be necessary. I have you fully committed to memory," Fallon murmured. "What did you think of the rest of the exhibit?"

"I think you made a stunning choice, leaving behind the vases of flowers and bowls of fruit. You have touched something primal that the general populace can appreciate."

Fallon gave a rueful smile. "Most people feel more comfortable with their emotions safely hanging over a fireplace."

"Is that it? You're giving them a chance to feel, but in a safe medium?"

"I believe that to be the main appeal, yes."

"And here I thought the attraction was the artist herself." He took a breath. "You look incredible. Happy, accomplished."

"Thank you. You look well, also. It was good to see you again, Bridge."

With that, she turned and started to walk away.

And Bridge knew he couldn't let her. He couldn't leave his emotions safely tucked away someplace. All his life, he'd thought he was the king of chance-taking. Suddenly, faced with the most important moment of his life, he was afraid. He tried to speak, but nothing came out. He tried again. "Fallon."

She glided back toward him.

This was her moment; her night of triumph. Did he risk spoiling the evening by pledging his suit? Yet, if he didn't make a move now, he could well lose her for all time.

"This series you're proposing. Would it eventually show the *Still Man in Motion* with a companion?"

"I'm not sure. I have difficulty envisioning you settling down with just one woman—and that's the only way I could complete the series to my satisfaction."

His eyes searched hers. Did she mean what he thought she meant? He took a step forward, and captured one of her hands in his. "You're wretchedly intimidating when you're this successful and popular, madam artist."

"Rather like you, when we first met. Sexy and self-confident and quite, quite arrogant. What happened to that cocksure self-confidence?"

"I had this amazing experience. A week outside of the usual parameters of life. A week of learning and sharing, as well as teaching."

"One can hardly remain unchanged after such an experience."

"Indeed." Bridge wished she were not wearing evening gloves; wished he could feel her skin against his. "Thus, I stand before you humbled. My bravado has deserted me. What I feel is too important to dismiss with false confidence."

"Oh?"

"You said before that our relationship was taboo. That people would disapprove, snigger about us behind our backs. You cared what people think. Do you still?"

"Oh, that," Fallon said. "That was simply an excuse."

"An excuse?"

"To make it easy to let you go."

"I didn't want you to let me go."

"I lacked the confidence to believe that, before."

"Do you believe me now?"

"Persuade me." There was a challenge in her eyes and in her smile.

"Can we find someplace to be alone?"

"I say we try." She leaned over and whispered, "I should warn you, I seem to have omitted certain items of underclothing beneath this gown."

Bridge caught her tightly in his arms. "I love you, Fallon. Marry me. Make me the happiest man in Boston."

"All in good time. For now, I know of this private spot where we can be alone. It's a tiny Juliet balcony with barely enough room for two. The moon is nearly full. I think it would be a romantic spot for a tryst."

"Say no more. Except . . ." He couldn't exactly beg her to return his declaration of love. "I have missed you so much."

"I have missed you, as well."

She whisked him out a back exit and up a narrow, winding flight of steps, to the next floor and the promised balcony. He took a breath. Boston lay spread before them, moonlight glittering on the roofs and chimneys. He could smell the harbor in the distance. Closer at hand, he could smell Fallon. Her hair. Her skin. The very woman-essence of her.

She came into his arms as if she had always been there, a perfect fit. Close to his heart. He stroked her hair. Even if she didn't love him, if she at least agreed to be with him . . .

She pulled off her gloves, rose onto tiptoe, and pressed a kiss to his lips. "You look so serious, Bridge."

He caught her hands in his and realized she no longer wore her dead husband's ring.

"I'm just realizing how lucky we are to have met. I've never loved anyone the way I love you." He couldn't stop himself from saying it aloud; it was time to face the potential rejection, to offer his heart on his sleeve.

"I love you, too," Fallon said. "I think I loved you the moment I set eyes on you. You were so alive and vital and sure of yourself—everything I wasn't. I didn't believe I had anything to offer, other than a week out of time."

"I don't know when I realized how much I love you. Maybe not until you sent me away. I tried to find you, and couldn't. That wretch Anna wouldn't tell me where you were."

"I'm here now."

"You're famous now. The toast of Boston."

She smiled teasingly. "As long as that's not the reason you claim to love me."

"I love you no matter who you are. No matter how others see you."

"I feel the same way toward you. I don't care a whit if people talk. Let them whisper that I've bought myself a young stud. All that matters is that we be together."

"Can we go back to your studio soon?"

"Why?"

"I'm thinking of experimenting. I'd like to invent an edible paint, and want you to be my first portrait."

"You mean apply the paint to my skin?"

"And slowly lick it off. Every delectable inch." He felt her shiver in his arms. "But first, there's a more pressing matter. I need to find out exactly what you have on beneath this frock." He slowly tugged up the hem of her skirt.

Fallon leaned against the railing, her eyes closed in rapture, moonlight bathing her face, as Bridge knelt before her . . . and discovered that there was, indeed, nothing to impede his adoration of her.

About the Author

Kathleen Lawless finds her inspiration on the beaches near her home in British Columbia. She believes chocolate and red wine are basic food groups, and knows firsthand that oysters are a natural aphrodisiac. The author of nine romances, she thinks the only thing better than romance is erotic romance.